Gun Law

GUN LAW

BRADFORD SCOTT

WHEELER
CHIVERS

This Large Print edition is published by Wheeler Publishing, Waterville, Maine, USA and by BBC Audiobooks Ltd, Bath, England.
Wheeler Publishing, a part of Gale, Cengage Learning.
A Walt Slade Western Series.

LIBRARY OF CONGRESS CATALOGING-IN-PUBLICATION DATA

Scott, Bradford, 1893–1975.
  Gun law / by Bradford Scott.
     p. cm. — (Wheeler Publishing large print western) (A Walt
  Slade western series)
     ISBN-13: 978-1-4104-2350-4 (softcover : alk. paper)
     ISBN-10: 1-4104-2350-6 (softcover : alk. paper)
     1. Texas Rangers—Fiction. 2. Texas—Fiction. 3. Large type
  books. I. Title.
  PS3537.C9265G85 2010
  813'.54—dc22   2009043675

BRITISH LIBRARY CATALOGUING-IN-PUBLICATION DATA AVAILABLE

Published in 2010 in the U.S. by arrangement with Golden West
Literary Agency.
Published in 2010 in the U.K. by arrangement with Golden West
Literary Agency.

U.K. Hardcover: 978 1 408 47828 8 (Chivers Large Print)
U.K. Softcover: 978 1 408 47829 5 (Camden Large Print)

Printed in the United States of America
1 2 3 4 5 6 7 14 13 12 11 10

GUN LAW

CHAPTER 1

"Sorry, sir, but the Rangers are not exactly a detective outfit, and hunting for missing persons, especially when they've been missing five or six years, is sort of out of our line.

"Of course, if you could show that the man in question met with foul play of some kind, the Rangers would do the best they could to run down the guilty persons and bring them to justice; but otherwise I don't see my way clear to assign men to the job, particularly when they are badly needed in other places right now."

Captain Jim McNelty, the famous commander of the far-flung Border Battalion of the Texas Rangers, spoke with finality, nodding his grizzled head in time with his words.

The comfortably fleshy, prosperous looking man sitting on the opposite side of the captain's table-desk was obviously disappointed. He leaned forward earnestly.

"Captain," he said, "I cannot prove that Robert Flint, my former business associate, met with foul play, although I am very much of the opinion that he did, but it is imperative that I ascertain his fate, one way or the other. I am prepared to pay a reward of ten thousand dollars for knowledge of his present whereabouts or proof of his demise."

"My men don't take —" the captain began.

The other interrupted, "I know, I know, the Rangers do not accept rewards. But Rangers who lose their lives in the performance of their duty sometimes leave dependents who lack adequate means of support. The ten thousand dollars could form the nucleus of a fund from which benefits would be paid to such needy dependents. Doesn't that strike you as something worthwhile?"

Captain McNelty remained silent, studying the other thoughtfully, apparently turning the proposition over carefully in his mind.

The stocky man in "store clothes" seemed to hesitate, then added with evident reluctance, "There's another phase to the matter I suppose I'd better mention."

"What's that, Mr. Duncan?" the captain asked.

"Robert Flint, prior to his disappearance, embezzled a large amount of money from the firm, and in addition broke open the office safe and purloined a good many thousand dollars reserved for payrolls and purchases."

"Hmm!" said the captain. "And did this occur after you moved your business from Tucson, Arizona, to Austin here in Texas?"

"That's right, sir," Duncan replied.

"That makes it a somewhat different proposition," observed the captain. "Now you are asking me to run down a criminal whose depredations were committed on Texas soil. Why didn't you say so in the first place?"

"I have no desire to prosecute Flint," Edward Duncan replied quietly. "At the time it happened, I felt — different; but since then, fate has been good to me and I have recouped the losses I suffered, losses that for a time threatened to ruin the business, and I have prospered greatly. And I freely admit that it was Flint's genius and remarkable knowledge of the principles of engineering that laid the foundation of my success. Why he did what he did is beyond my comprehension, but I believe he gambled heavily and that can be the ruination of a man. Anyhow, he went crooked and very nearly wiped me out. That's water over the dam, however, and I would not care much where Flint is, if he still lives, or what became of him, were it not for the fact that there are certain large interests I wish to dispose of and it is important that I know for certain whether Flint is living or dead, in order to take the necessary steps to clear the properties. The knowledge would enable me to avoid expensive delays and much costly litigation. And, I reiterate, I will gladly pay well for it."

Captain McNelty thoughtfully tugged his mustache, a speculative gleam in his cold blue eyes. Duncan seemed to experience a sense of relief from speaking freely.

"The time I had running you down, Captain," he chuckled. "Having made up my mind that you were the man who could help me, I took the train to Alice, where I understood you had your headquarters, only to learn you had just been transferred way over here near the Big Ben country. Seemed fortunate in a way, though, for this locality is not very far from where Flint was, I believe, last seen. I traced his movements as best I was able, but my operatives finally completely lost the track and gave up. So I came to you."

Captain McNelty nodded. "Just been here in Patricio a few days," he said. "Considerable trouble along the Border right now that needs attention. Only a few of my boys here yet." He glanced out the window toward the lights that twinkled through the deepening dusk.

"I'm hungry," he announced, rising to his feet. "Suppose you and I walk over to Brighton's place and tie onto a little something to eat? Then we'll discuss this business some more. I can always think better with a full plate in front of me."

Duncan offered no objection and they left the office together. A couple of minutes' walk along the busy main street of Patricio brought them to the big saloon and restaurant run by Packrat Brighton. They took a table and gave their orders to a waiter.

The businessman from Austin tactfully refrained from re-opening the discussion while the orders were being filled. He gazed with interest on the, to him, novel scene, noting the long bar crowded with cowhands and ranchers, the roulette wheels and occupied poker tables, the girls on the dance floor.

"Say!" he exclaimed, "that fellow at the end of the bar certainly can sing!"

Catpain McNelty glanced at the man in question, who was in his late twenties, possibly a little older. He wore the conventional garb of the cow country — faded overalls, dark shirt, its somber hue relieved by the bright flash of the handkerchief looped about his sinewy throat, close-fitting shotgun chaps and high-healed half-boots of softly tanned leather and well scuffed. The broad-brimmed hat was pushed back from a wide forehead singularly white in contrast to his lean, deeply bronzed cheeks, revealing thick black hair. His eyes were rather long and of a very clear gray. They were cold eyes fringed by extraordinarily long and thick black lashes, but there were little devils of laughter dancing in their depths. His mouth was a trifle wide with a grin-quirking at the corners that somewhat relieved the tinge of sternness, almost fierceness evinced by the hawk nose above and the lean, powerful chin and jaw beneath. He was a tall man, more than six feet, and the breadth of his shoulders and the depth of his chest matched his height.

Filled double cartridge belts encircled his lean waist and from the carefully worked and oiled cut-out holsters protruded the plain black butts of heavy guns.

The tall "cowboy's" slim, sun-tanned

fingers swept over the strings of a small guitar he had borrowed from the orchestra leader with a touch as delicate as the whisper of the wind in the prairie grasses, and to the soft accompaniment he sang a lilting melody in a voice that was like golden wine gushing into a crystal goblet.

The noise at the bar hushed and the roulette wheels ceased to whir as the great metallic baritone-bass pealed and thundered to the unpainted rafters of the big room. The dealers held their decks and the dance-floor girls gathered in silent groups, their eyes fixed on the tall bronze-faced singer of dreams.

With a crash of chords and a last exultant note the music ceased. The singer grinned with a flash of white, even teeth at the roar of applause and raised his glass in acknowledgment. Catching Captain McNelty's eye, he nodded; the captain nodded back.

"You know him?" asked Edward Duncan.

"Yes, I know him, and know of him," McNelty replied. "Name's Slade — Walt Slade. The Mexicans call him *El Halcon* — that means The Hawk in English. Ambled into town day before yesterday."

"The Hawk!" remarked Duncan. "Hmm! he looks it. Like one of those big glitter-eyed fellows you see in the mountains, that will tackle anything, including an eagle, if necessary. Mexicans are good at giving people names that fit them. Cowhand, isn't he?"

"Guess he is, when he's working at it," conceded Captain Jim. "One thing I'd say sure for certain, he's the singingest man in Texas."

"I agree with you there," Duncan declared heartily. "And he's certainly an interesting looking person."

"I'll call him over," the captain suggested, and did so with an imperative gesture before the other could protest.

Walt Slade crossed the room with lithe steps, bringing the guitar with him, his fingers still breathing over the strings.

"Sit down where I can keep an eye on you," said Captain Jim. "Trouble just follows you around. Meet Mr. Edward Duncan from Austin; he likes your music."

Slade smiled acknowledgment and the two men shook hands.

"And now, Mr. Duncan," said Captain Jim as he fell to work on his filled plate, "suppose you go over from the beginning what you told me at the office. I want all the details so that I'll be sure to get the straight of it."

Duncan hesitated, glancing questioningly

14

at Slade.

"Oh, Walt's all right," said the captain, interpreting the glance. "He doesn't talk out of turn, I'll say that much for him. Besides, he won't have any interest in the business."

Thus reassured, Duncan repeated all he had told the captain, adding a few additional details, while Captain Jim plied a busy knife and fork.

"Let's see, now," observed the captain when Duncan paused. "As I understand, the man Robert Flint was last seen on the edge of the Tinto Desert, headed northwest, that right?"

"Yes," replied Duncan. "He had a prospector's outfit and was headed for the Tinto Hills on the other side of the desert."

"Any notion about where?"

"So far as I was able to learn, he was making for the hills near where a mining town called Coffin is now located; but that was before the town was built, I gather. It seems they had a gold strike near there not long after Robert Flint vanished into the hills."

"Nobody saw him after he went into the desert?"

"It would appear no one saw him after the storekeeper in a little town on the edge of the desert, from whom he bought his outfit."

"How did the storekeeper know he was Flint?"

"He didn't, of course," answered Duncan. "But when I described Flint as a man slightly under six feet tall and broad-shouldered, with very piercing blue eyes, black hair and a black beard, he distinctly recalled the wandering prospector and declared the description fitted him perfectly. That added to the fact that I know Flint was headed in that direction convinces me that the prospector was Robert Flint and no other. So far as I've been able to learn, it appears the storekeeper was the last man to see Flint alive."

Captain McNelty nodded thoughtfully and asked a few more questions relative to Flint's physical appearance and known habits, which Duncan answered to the best of his ability.

Walt Slade appeared to pay scant attention to the conversation. He played softly on his guitar and his gray eyes roved over the big room.

Other eyes roved, also — in his direction. Particularly the sloe eyes of a lithe dancing girl with a red flower in her black hair who stood talking with a couple of swarthy men near the dance floor. Abruptly, with an impatient shrug of her slim shoulders she turned her back on them and sauntered across the room, glancing casually to right and left. She arrived at Slade's table by a circuitous route and paused as if by accident. Slade smiled up at her and she started to speak.

With a curse, the larger of the two swarthy men charged across the room. Big as he was, he moved like a catamount and his huge hand was reaching for the girl even as she turned at the sound of his boots, her face blanching.

Without any appearance of haste, Walt Slade laid the guitar on the table and came to his feet in one supple movement. Slim fingers like rods of nickel steel gripped the big man's wrist and whirled him about with no apparent effort.

"Better head back where you came from, *amigo*," El Halcon's musical voice drawled.

Sputtering curses, the man lunged with vicious fists. Slade weaved lithely aside and hit him, his hand appearing to travel but a few inches.

The big man seemed to acquire wings. His feet left the floor and an instant later his back landed on it with a crash that shook the room and set the hanging lamps to dancing. He twitched and lay still.

At the same instant Slade's right hand moved in a flickering blur. A long black gun whipped from its sheath, smoke wisping from its muzzle as it cleared leather. The hanging lamps danced again to the boom of the report.

Across the room the second swarthy man screamed shrilly and gripped his bullet-smashed hand with crimsoning fingers. The knife he had poised to throw tinkled to the floor. Yells and whoops shook the air, and the crackling and splintering of chairs as men dived frantically behind posts or under tables.

Packrat Brighton came pounding across the room bawling cuss words and questions, his lookout and a couple of floor men beside him. A terse word from Captain McNelty and they hauled the unconscious man out the front door, hustling his wounded companion after him. Slade holstered his gun, picked up the guitar and resumed playing.

Edward Duncan had good ears, and as he mopped his suddenly damp brow with a shaking hand, he heard a voice mutter in low tones to a companion in the milling crowd, "Those darn fools musta never have heard of El Halcon, or they wouldn't have tried it. I tell you that owlhoot hellion is plumb pizen!"

"Ain't nobody knows for sure he's an outlaw," objected a second voice. "Sure ain't never been thrown in jail, so far as anybody ever heard tell. Sure he's got killings to his credit, but the gents he plowed under were always mighty ornery specimens and he just saved rope for some sheriff."

"Maybe he ain't an owlhoot," replied the second voice as they started to move away, "but it's mighty seldom a feller who rides a straight trail can handle a gun like he does. And look how he wears those irons! Billy the Kid and King Fisher and Doc Holliday always hung their holsters that way. See Captain McNelty is keeping a close watch on him. Wouldn't be surprised, now that Captain Jim's set up headquarters here, that El Halcon trails his twine out of this section before long."

Captain McNelty fixed his cold glance on Slade. "Feller," he said, "someday you're going to get your comeuppance because of some darn fool girl making sheep's eyes at you. You'd ought to get some of your teeth knocked out or your nose busted crooked or something like that, for your own protection." With a snort at the twinkle dancing in Slade's eyes, he turned back to his table companion.

"I'll do what I can for you, Mr. Duncan," he said. "Yes, according to what you learned of his last known movements, it would appear your man disappeared somewhere near where the mining town of Coffin now is. They've been having trouble at Coffin of late. Seems a rather dubious character named Graves has been rising to prominence there and is sort of taking over the running of the town. I may have to station a Ranger there and I'll tell him to keep an eye open for Flint."

Walt Slade beckoned the leader, handed him his guitar with a word of thanks and rose to his feet.

"Well, *adios,* gents," he drawled. "I think I'll do a little riding tonight."

"A good idea," Captain McNelty agreed dryly. "This pueblo could stand a little session of peace and quiet."

El Halcon sauntered toward the swinging doors, seeming to drift across the floor rather than walk, and men respectfully made way for him. At the doors he turned and waved his hand to Duncan and McNelty. With a flash of his white teeth and a laughing gleam of his gray eyes, he vanished into the night. Edward Duncan drew a long breath.

"Captain," he said, "judging by what I just

gathered from an overheard conversation, that man strays pretty close to the outside fringe of the law; but it is my respectful opinion that you ought to get hold of him, straighten him out and — make him one of your Rangers."

"Mr. Duncan, you may have a pretty good notion there," agreed Captain Jim, sober as a judge.

CHAPTER 2

Walt Slade, humming softly to himself, was getting the rig on Shadow, his great black horse, when a tall figure loomed in the stable door.

"Well, what do you think of it?" asked Captain McNelty.

"A queer yarn," Slade answered. "But this country is full of queer yarns, with every now and then one solidly foundationed on fact. Which could be the case with Robert Flint. He could still be alive and hanging around Coffin, as Duncan seems to believe, but I'd say it's unlikely. If he went into the Tinto Hills about five years back, in my opinion he had a mighty good chance to stay there. Old Chief Laughing Bear and his renegade Apaches were hanging out in the Tintos in those days. Used to raid the cattle ranches to the east from them. Laughing Bear hated whites and killed every one he could catch. His favorite game was wandering prospectors and hunters. Not long afterward, Uncle Sam's cavalry killed Laughing Bear and most of his braves and packed the rest off to a reservation. Yes, it is quite probable that Robert Flint's bones are moldering back somewhere in the hills with a bullet hole in his skull and an arrow head or two in his ribs."

"Well, Flint is a side issue, after all," said Captain Jim. "That fund for the dependents of killed Rangers Duncan proposed to set up is attractive and I'd be pleased if there developed a chance to tie onto it. Seeing as you're headed for Coffin, anyhow, you can keep your eyes open for Flint. But your real meat is Pancho Graves and his bunch. Not much doubt but that he's an ornery specimen even though nobody has ever been able to pin anything serious on him. It's sure for certain that he goes in for smuggling, but so long as he just dealt in harmless merchandise nobody aside from the Customs men paid much attention to him. Different, though, if he's mixed up in this gun running to Mexico that has the capital by the ears. That could have serious repercussions for Texas if it was allowed to go unchecked.

So find out if Graves really is mixed up in it. If he is, drop a loop on him. I've heard a rumor — haven't been able to verify it yet — that he had a big hand in having the county seat moved to Coffin and in getting a sheriff elected who he's friendly with. Can't say for sure about it although I got my information from a pretty reliable source. I wouldn't have given the hellion credit for that much brains, but that's the way I heard it. You should be able to find out for sure when you get there."

"Something like the Curly Bill Brocius, Johnny Behan combine over in Cochise County, Arizona, a few years back," Slade commented.

"Could be," Captain Jim agreed. "Well, see what you can do. Keep the fool women away from you and you'll be all right," Captain Jim, a confirmed bachelor of sixty and better, concluded caustically. Slade grinned and made no commitments.

Walt Slade rode west for two nights and a day, then north across the Tinto Desert. A silvery shimmer of moonlight softened the harsh outlines of crag and chimney rock and distorted cactus and changed the sinister scene to a fairyland of weird beauty. Slade's tall horse, black as the shadows of the night itself, seemed to barely touch the sands with dainty hoofs that aroused only a whisper of sound. He appeared utterly tireless despite the fact that this was his third night on the trail with very little rest during the entire period.

His rider also looked little the worse for wear except for a slight weariness of the steady gray eyes and a tightening of the firm mouth. Nevertheless there was a note of relief in his voice as he spoke to the big horse.

"Well, we should be sighting the lights of Coffin before very long now, you old grass-burner," he said. "It's about time! The next time I want to go someplace in a hurry, I'll hitch me up a couple of snails."

Shadow snorted his indignation at such libel and Slade tickled his ribs with his spurs until the black horse fairly danced with rage and reached for his rider's leg with gleaming teeth that missed their mark apparently by a miracle. They ambled on, Slade chuckling merrily and Shadow appearing to grin appreciation of the joke; the pair understood each other.

To the left, only a few hundred yards distant, was a jumble of "badland" buttes and chimney rocks which stretched up from the south to end a quarter of a mile farther on toward the unseen lights of Coffin. Slade was diagonaling toward the outcropping, expecting to pass around its northernmost straggle on his route to the town. Each whispering beat of his horse's irons brought him nearer to the grotesque fangs of shadow. Abruptly Slade's chuckle ceased; Shadow pricked his ears inquiringly. From the gloom of the broken ground had come an echoing beat, multiplied many times.

El Halcon was instantly alert, for he catalogued that vague drumming as the thud of hoofs on the harder soil of the badlands. Sounded like a bunch going someplace in a hurry, which was strange for this time of night. Could hardly be a cattle drive coming through that mess of rocks and gulleys. A funny place for anybody to be coming out of. Of course, it could be just a troop of cowhands headed for town. But what the devil were they doing in that ungodly terrain to the west? The cow ranches of the section were to the east of Coffin, or so he had been told. He strained his eyes to catch a glimpse of the mysterious riders before they saw him.

The shadows ahead abruptly came to life as a score or so of horses bulged from among the rocks. Slade's keen eyes told him at once that less than half the critters were mounted, the other were heavily-laden pack animals. He stared in surprise at the queer cavalcade, then hurled his body sideways in the saddle. Just in time he had caught the quick gleam of shifted steel.

Slade heard the bullet yell past his head and saw the red flicker from the gun barrel at the same instant. His knees clamped the black horse and Shadow went into a weaving, shifting dance.

Again the gun barked, and another slug whined past. Then, with a rattling crackle, several sixes let go at once.

Walt Slade's mind worked with the lightning speed and precision born of long and intimate association with danger. This was no significant warning to "mind your own business!" on the part of the smuggling or widelooping outfit; those shots were meant to kill. Behind him was a wide stretch of moon-bathed desert; to whirl his horse and flee would be but to offer a perfect target for the drygulchers who would halt their own horses and take deliberate aim. Nor could he hope to stand and shoot it out with nearly half a scorn gunmen. There was but one course for him to follow — verging on deliberate suicide, but with a tiny chance of success.

"Trail, Shadow!" he boomed, leaning low

over the black's neck, dropping the reins and jerking his guns from their holsters.

Straight for the dark group raced the great horse, his hoofs thundering, sand and loose boulders shooting out behind his spurning irons. On either side of his tossing head poured streams of flame and smoke, answering shot for shot the reddish flickers toward which he rushed.

The drygulchers yelled their consternation as the living thunderbolt of death and destruction tore at them. Their plunging horses, unwilling to face those blazing guns, scattered from Shadow's path. Bullets hissed and crackled past horse and rider, but the drygulchers were firing wildly with no chance to aim. Before they knew it The Hawk was in their midst, slashing viciously with the heavy barrels of his empty guns.

Slade heard steel crunch against flesh and bone, felt jarring shocks to his wrists and arms, had a single glimpse of a reeling dark face and gleaming eyes limned by the flash of a gun. Then he was through the cursing, yelling stampede and racing for the protection of the rocks. With a movement like the flicker of a sunbeam on a ripple he holstered the smoking Colts, jerked his heavy Winchester from the saddle boot and turned in the saddle. His gray eyes, cold as snow-dusted ice, glanced along the sights, his finger squeezed the trigger.

Slade did not hear the spiteful crack of his own rifle. The report was drowned in a crashing roar of sound, his eyes were dazzled by a flare of yellowish flame and he was all but hurled from the saddle by a screeching hurricane-blast of wind that tore past, whipping his clothes, beating his face with sand and gravel.

Shadow stumbled, floundered, recovered as Slade's hand tightened the reins; he darted between the buttes, squealing with fright. Behind sounded an awful scream of agony and a succession of dull thuds.

Blinded, deafened, Slade rode on, trusting to the instinct and sure-footedness of his horse, his ears ringing, flashes of lurid light still storming before his eyes. He was nearly a mile from the scene of the encounter and deep amid a jumble of spires and towers that loomed black against the moon-white sky when he pulled his blowing horse to a halt in a black patch of shadow and sat listening intently.

No sound broke the stillness of the night. There was no movement among the buttes; but he waited many minutes, straining ears and eyes, before he turned Shadow's head and sent him slowly back the way he had come, pulling up frequently to peer and listen.

Guns reloaded and ready, every faculty at razor-edge sharpness, Slade pulled the black horse to a halt at the edge of the moonlight desert. Again he sat for long minutes, alert for some sign of life, and saw and heard nothing. With a whispered word of command he dropped the split reins to the ground and swung from the saddle. Once more he paused, then, reassured by the continued stillness, he glided forward on foot, as silent and unseen as the faint wind breathing across the sands. Beside a sheltering rock he crouched and surveyed the scene of battle.

Nothing was to be seen of the drygulchers. Over to one side, grotesque in the moonlight, lay the shattered body of a horse. Another lay a little farther on, just beyond a deep hole scooped in the sand. Something nearby reflected a gleam of the moonlight and Slade's attention fixed on it. By degrees he realized it was the shoe of a horse, but there was no horse attached to the shoe — only the hoof and a splintered fragment of leg bone.

"And that must have come off the poor cayuse packing the box of dynamite my rifle bullet hit," muttered the Ranger.

In the moonlight he could see a long distance and, sure that none of the trigger-happy gunmen had remained on the scene, he examined the blasted bodies of the horses. Their packs had been removed and even the brands cut out. Evidently the horsemen had been careful that nothing remained which would tie them up to what had happened. If any had been killed, and Slade thought that only by a miracle could all have escaped the blast, they had been packed off by their companions who remained alive.

With minute care, Slade quartered the ground, ranging from the shadow of the buttes to beyond where he had first sighted the troop. He was about to give up the search when for a second time a gleam of metal caught his eye. A moment later he picked up a short, heavy drill with a well sharpened and somewhat flattened cutting edge. He recognized it as the kind of tool used for drilling holes in rock to receive dynamite cartridges. Which was interesting and a bit puzzling.

Just what sort of an outfit had he stumbled onto, he wondered. He had never heard of dynamite and drills being smuggled across the Mexican Border, at least not coming north. A bank-robbing bunch might employ dynamite, but they certainly would not use rock drills to break into a safe. Greatly intrigued, Slade wondered if he could pick up the trail left by the bunch.

Finding nothing more of interest, he mounted Shadow and rode slowly, scanning the ground with great care. For a while he followed the trail easily enough. It veered away from where he knew Coffin must be located and flowed toward the dark loom of the Tinto Hills. Soon, however, the combination of dying moonlight and the increasing roughness of the ground made following the track no longer possible and Slade turned Shadow's head toward Coffin once more, puzzling over the meaning of the strange experience.

It seemed certain that the caravan was not headed for town. He wondered where in blazes they came from out of that mess of rocks which stretched southward almost to the Rio Grande.

"Well, horse, it looks like our little amble to this section may turn out quite interesting, even if we don't manage to get a line on the ten thousand dollars worth of gent Mr. Duncan was gabbing about. Not that I had much notion that we would get a chance to tie onto him. Very likely the hills got him, just as they have gotten lots of others. If he'd been alive and roaming around there he would have been very apt to show up at Coffin after they made the big gold strike and started the town — most any prospector would have. I gather the strike was made just about the time, or shortly after, he went into the hills. Funny, isn't it, horse, that right in the same section one man will find a fortune and another a grave!"

Shadow's answering snort seemed to observe pointedly, "There's plenty of room in those hills for another or two." Slade chuckled and was inclined to agree.

"But you don't need to make it so darn personal," he protested. "Well, looks like right ahead is where we're headed for."

They had topped a rise and in the distance ahead lay a cluster of golden stars set much lower than their fellows in the moon-washed vault above.

"Yes, that's Coffin or we've been traveling in the wrong direction for the past few days. Let's go, feller, I'm hungry."

With brooding eyes he gazed at the widespread twinkle of lights that steadily drew nearer, wondering idly what the scene had been like before man arrived to rob the hills of their treasure and build the town at the desert's edge. He could not know what happened only a few short years before.

CHAPTER 3

Two men stood in the vestibule of the bleak Tinto Hills. At their backs, rolling southward to the distant Rio Grande, stretched the arid desolation of the terrible Tinto Desert, fanged with spires and chimney rocks and buttes fantastically carved throughout untold ages by the tireless fingers of the wind-driven sand. To the east, beyond a narrow strip of desert and broken hill ground, was rangeland where grew the needle and wheat grasses, and curly mesquite rich in the distilled spirit of the hot sun and sweet rain of the dry country — an oasis in the vast and almost universal expanse of cactus, greasewood and sage.

The two men, however, were not interested in the rich prairie where thousands of fat cattle fed. Their gaze was fixed on the inhospitable jumble of towers and craggy battlements that were the van of the gaunt hills fanging into the brassy-blue Texas sky. This region of mesas, faults and escarpments consisted of the surviving fragment of an older plain that had been worn down by wind and sun and rain beating upon it for eons. It was grim and forbidding as the walled and turreted treasure hold of some feudal robber-baron or pirate king.

And even as did the moldering bones of those who hid the treasure at behest of their lord and had their lips sealed to eternal silence as a reward, the sinister hills could also show their quota of bleaching skeletons of those who had sought to penetrate their fastnesses and tear a golden secret from their stony breasts.

For the hills guarded a treasure hold, only waiting the rip of the miner's pick, in the right place, to pour forth a rich flood. But Death himself guarded their secret and there was little in their bleak poverty appearance to warrant such a belief. Coronado and his Spaniards in hauberk and plate of proof gave them but an incurious glance. Mexican marauder and American adventurer had seen in them only a refuge and place of hiding, or a stronghold for depredating bands that swept down upon the rich rangeland to the east and retired to their holes and hideaways with ill-gotten gains. Comanche and Apache lurked there when in flight from blue-clad cavalry men or the even sterner and more feared "Gentlemen in the White Hats," the Rangers. The Tinto Hills were sanctuary for those whose deeds made a mockery of the words mercy and forgiveness.

But all the while the wealth of the Seven Cities of Cibola was there. There and waiting. There were prospectors who gleaned an inkling of the truth, and who left their bones amid the dry washes and the crags or, gaunt and starving, staggered back to the open country with a bellyful of the hills, and nothing else.

The two men knew all this and it was not surprising that they hesitated, staring at the forbidding terrain, sensing its malevolent threat.

They were men of somewhat above average height, broad of shoulder, deep of chest, with sinewy, active figures and faces bronzed by wind and sun. The mouth of each was firm and hard-set, as befitted men who were wont to set their faces against danger.

But there the resemblance ended. The older man, whose face was deeply-lined, had tawny hair streaked with gray and sunny brown eyes. His companion's hair was black, his eyes blue and what lines there were in his face were not those traced by the kindly fingers of the passing years but scoured out by the raking nails of hard pleasure.

The two men stood at the forks of a wide

dry wash whose sides were thickly grown with grass and flowering weeds. There were ocotillos with tall wands, green and curving, spraying from a single central root. Mescal plants, green and yellow, shot more than a score of feet into the air, their starry white blooms dazzling against the pale sky. Chollas raised their crooked arms and brandished their needle-like spines. Thorny chaparral grew in dense thickets along the floor of the wash, gnarled roots exposed by the tearing rush of water during the infrequent storms. The thick interlacing of roots and branches served to check the run-off of water. It also presented an unpleasant barrier to the progress of man and beast.

The left fork of the draw was the more heavily overgrown, the right being comparatively free of the hampering brush.

The two men were not partners, having met by chance in the course of the desert crossing. They had remained together for a period for company's sake, with a tacit agreement that they would separate upon reaching the hills and prospecting ground. Now they were at the parting of the ways. Behind each stood his loaded burro with drooping head and hypocritical air of meekness.

"All right, feller," magnanimously offered

the tawny-haired man, "you take your pick and go whichever way you figure is best."

The younger man hesitated, his blue eyes narrowing. He glanced at the more difficult left arm of the wash and turned quickly from it. He was about to speak when the burro behind him brayed raucously.

As if snapped into action by the sound, a bird darted from beneath a mesquite bush and scuttled up the right arm of the wash. It was a big bird, fully two feet in length, with stiff brown and whitish striped plumage, a conspicuous head crest, powerful legs and feet and a long graduated tail held at a cocky angle.

The blue-eyed man cursed viciously as the chaparral cock, or road runner, whizzed up the wash at amazing speed. He glared after it resentfully and shook his fist as it vanished amid the brush. Then he turned to the left with decision written on his angry face.

"I wouldn't follow the trail of that scoot-tailed hellion anywhere!" he announced. "The blasted things are always bad luck to me. You take the easy way, feller, and I'll hit the brush."

Still rumbling curses, he turned left and stormed off through the growth, the burro trotting after him. His companion laughed merrily, his sunny eyes twinkling with amusement, and entered the other arm of the draw.

The blue-eyed man crashed on through the brush, following the winding course of the wash, paying scant heed to his surroundings. Finally, however, his anger spent itself and the hardness of the going forced him to slacken his speed. From time to time he paused to narrowly examine ledges or outcroppings or bits of float washed down from the upper draw, scowling at the gray cliffs and shaking his head in disapproval. He discovered nothing of particular interest during the afternoon, and evening found him making his camp for the night on one of a series of broad benches which the wash laboriously climbed like a tired snake going up a flight of stairs.

He cooked his simple meal and lay down to sleep beside his dying fire. And from behind a boulder on the edge of the bench above, savage eyes glared from beneath a dingy white turban with an eagle feather set low against the dirty cloth. As the shadows deepened the Apache scout crept away into the darkness, rifle cradled in the crook of his arm, moccasined feet silent on the stones, with only the tiny click of his necklace of bear claws to mark his going.

The tired prospector slept soundly, but as

he slept a devil's ring closed about him. In the first gray light of dawn the tethered burro raised an inquiring head, then dropped it to the grass again as a faint clicking sound ceased to annoy his sensitive ears.

The silent dawn cast its red mantle over the lonely hills. A bird sang a tentative note. A little wind stirred the grasses and shook from them a myriad of dew gems. The prospector yawned, threw his blankets aside. Lithe, powerful, he sprang to his feet, flexing his long arms above his head. Then he hurled himself headlong to the ground again.

Only the keenest of eyes and marvelous coordination of mind and muscle saved him from the storm blast of death that burst from the surrounding rocks. His quick glance had caught the tell-tale glint of a rifle barrel as an Apache shifted it slightly to assure truer aim. Over him screeched the slugs from the Indian guns.

The burro went down, kicking and squealing, twitched for a moment and was still. The prospector rolled and squirmed, bullets snapping all about him, until he was behind and almost beneath the body of the dead animal. His rifle was beyond reach, but his heavy sixgun was in its holster. Grim, deadly, he answered the Indians shot for shot. Blood streamed down his face, but his thin lips writhed back from his set teeth and he snarled defiance at the swarthy killers.

Writhing through the brush like a snake, a lean and stringy brave gained a point from where he could obtain a clear shot. His beady eyes glinted behind the sights, his finger tightened on the trigger. He fired point-blank just as the victim, warned by some uncanny second sight, whirled about.

The prospector screamed, writhing and twitching on the ground. The Apaches surged forward with whoops of triumph. The whoops changed to yells of alarm and a shriek of agony as the prospector, his face a mask of blood through which his teeth gleamed whitely, suddenly surged to his feet, sixgun blazing.

But the odds were too great; guns banged, hatchets lashed out and the prospector went down under an avalanche of bodies. A scalping knife glittered in the first sunlight, but before it could descend to slice out a neat circle of scalp the size of a silver dollar and a tuft of hair, a watching outpost screeched a warning.

Whirling at that urgent cry, the Indians glared down the draw. Along a lower bench horsemen were urging their mounts at top speed. The rising sun gleamed on blue cloth and brass buttons and on the hilts of sabres. Puffs of smoke mushroomed from the tight ranks, the reports were like the crackle of burning sticks.

The Indians hesitated no longer. Ignoring their victim they fled among the rocks like rabbits, came to where their wiry little mustangs were tethered and scrambled onto their backs. Off they went, "hoo-hooing" through the brush, and after them thundered the cavalry troop that for days and nights had been searching for this very band of marauders.

The soldiers had not witnessed the stark drama enacted on the upper bench and had glimpsed the Indians only when swerving around a shoulder of stone. So they rode on after their quarry.

And on the lofty bench the prospector lay motionless with his bloody face buried in the grass. While high in the brightening sky, tiny black specks grew larger as the great condor-vultures that can scent death for miles swooped lower and lower over the still forms of man and beast.

Tom Ware, the tawny-haired man, went on up the right arm of the wash after his ill-starred companion left him, and discovered the great Last Nugget gold mine, as rich a quartz ledge as Texas had yet known. Sitting beneath a shattered outcropping beside the claim he had staked after laboriously writing out his "Notices," with fragments of gold wired and studded ore scattered over his lap and a light of quiet happiness in his kindly eyes, he dreamed wondrous dreams and saw visions of prosperity and content for others beside himself.

From out on the desert the dry wash looks like the gaping mouth of a rattlesnake with the fangs reared. On the jutting lower jaw of the "snake," Tom Ware built a town. With a macabre sense of humor he named it "Coffin," having in mind the bleached bones and grinning skulls so frequently encountered back in the hills. And the roaring mining town proceeded to live up to its name.

In the beginning Tom Ware ran the town with a firm and just hand. His word was final on all matters of policy and behaviour — for a while.

That is, it was "final" until some time after the advent of Cole Young.

Young was a deep-chested, powerful man with long arms and a hard mouth. He had grizzled hair and his face was marred by the unsightly puckered scars of ill-healed wounds. Part of the bridge of his nose was gone and one eyelid lay flat over an empty socket. The remaining eye, however, gleamed with a fierce and bitter energy, as if the whole turbulent soul of the man were bursting through that single narrow cranny.

Young arrived in Coffin shortly after the big Last Nugget and the other mines, some of them owned by Tom Ware and his associates and others by fortunate late-comers, began operating full blast. He opened a small saloon and gambling house and prospered.

The Square Deal, Young's place, was a modest establishment — in the beginning — but it was unique in its relation to the average Border-mining-cattle town *cantina*. Young sold only the best whiskey, he ran square games and his dance-floor girls were good looking and he required them to play fair. It was not strange, therefore, that patronage flocked his way and he soon found it necessary to seek larger quarters.

It seemed strange to many, however, that the hardest characters of both Coffin and the surrounding country should seek out Young's place. Young's explanation was simple.

"Those fellows take big chances in getting their money," he was wont to say. "They risk hot lead and the noose-end of a rope for their dinero. Do you think they want to spend it in places where they're liable to get flim-flammed by scheming women or robbed by a crooked wheel? They don't! And they like the kind of whiskey that doesn't leave them shaky and bleary-eyed the next morning. When you carry your life in your trigger finger you're apt to be sort of particular about that. See?"

Whether folks "saw" or not, the fact remained, indisputable — Cole Young prospered and gradually became a power in the town that rioted with lusty life on the rattlesnake's lip. Tom Ware continued to wield strong influence in the town itself, but in surrounding Tinto County, Young's influence was greater.

Tom Ware was an honest and kindly man with a great respect for law and order, but he was no politician. His schooling had been limited to the eighth grade. Cole Young, on the other hand, was a politician, an able and adroit one, and he was a man of more than average education. Young knew how to play his cards to the best advantage and how to corral votes when needed, especially among an element that Tom Ware scorned and with which he would have no dealings. He did not dream splendid dreams as did Tom Ware, but he had vision and quickly realized that the man who could control the questionable characters of the town and the surrounding country and cause them to do his bidding could control Coffin and Tinto County.

Working subtly and unobtrusively, Young proceeded to do just that. Within three years he had extended his influence and consolidated his power to such an extent that he was able to get John Blount, one of his associates, elected sheriff of the county. Blount immediately appointed deputies who also were friendly to Cole Young. Tom Ware still controlled the town council and got his choice for town marshal appointed. Cole Young had his eye on that post, too, and the councilmanic election was not far off. Meanwhile, Sheriff Blount enjoyed full authority in the surrounding country. Nobody had ever been able to prove anything against fat John Blount; but folks thought plenty, and it was a well known fact that Blount had the outlaw vote corraled. He and notorious Pancho Graves had been known to drink together in Coffin, which was far and away the largest town in the county.

Coffin, for all its hilariousness, had from its inception been comparatively law-abiding, but Tinto County as a whole was something else again. It was woolly for even a Border county.

Cole Young hated Tom Ware, that was an open secret, and Ware, a stickler for principles and an exponent of law and order, had scant use for the one-eyed owner of the Square Deal. The feud between them smoldered and it was freely predicted that the time would come when it would break to the surface.

"Then," old-timers were wont to predict darkly, "then look out! Hell will be a-poppin' and the Devil to pay, and no pitch hot!"

Whether they were right, only time would tell, but there was no doubt but Coffin was changing from a fairly orderly mining town to something radically different.

Had, indeed, already changed greatly from the decent, respectable community Tom Ware had envisioned as he sat alone in the Tinto Hills with fragments of gold-bearing ore strewn across his lap. All of which Ware was forced to reluctantly admit. What would not have been countenanced two years before was now all too prevalent. Powder smoke was mingling with tobacco smoke, and the glitter of the spangles on the short skirts of the dance-floor girls was rivaled by the gleam of drawn knives.

CHAPTER 4

Such was the town into which Walt Slade rode as the western crags pulled the dying moon down behind their frowning battlements and drowned her in a flood of her own silver tears. The lights of turbulent Chaparro Street were winking out and the few doors along the main thoroughfare that were ever locked were closing. Drunken men reeled along the board sidewalks shouting and cursing. From luridly-lighted windows came the high-pitched, raucous laughter of women whose lips were too red and whose eyes were too bright. Somewhere in a dark doorway a wounded man moaned through the blood that gurgled in his slashed throat. On the sodden, whiskey-soaked sawdust of a deserted dive, something that had once been a man lay very still, its unseeing eyes glaring up at the smoky ceiling. Guns cracked now and then as some bleary reveller tried to shoot out the stars. Cards still slithered over the green cloth of tables with shaded lights. Roulette wheels whirred with a monotonous drone. Despite the nearness of the dawn, weary bartenders sloshed whiskey into ready glasses. There would still be more than one deadly fight before the sunlight turned the desert sands to shimmering bronze and molten gold. Coffin was living up to its name.

"Yes, she's a salty pueblo," Walt Slade told his horse as he turned its head toward a little side-street livery stable. "Looks like you and I ought to do a little business here."

A sleepy but good-natured stable keeper admitted them and answered Slade's question as to accommodations for himself.

"There's a room above the stalls you can sleep in," he said. "Finest 'commodations in town," he added with a drowsy chuckle, "horse trough in the back with nice running water you can take a bath in if you're so minded, fresh straw tick to pound your ear on and a first rate eating house just around the corner, run by a Mexican a hundred and seventy years old — I'll knock off the hundred — but he's sure got more wrinkles than a worried prune. Dishes out prime chuck, though, and is a good Injun. Call him Manuel and he'll come a-running."

Slade was awakened the following morning by yells and shots and clattering hoofs. He dressed, descended the stairs and asked the stable keeper what all the commotion was about.

"Some of Pancho Graves' hellions riding into town," explained the keeper. "They

48

always kick up a ruckus like that just for the devil of it. Graves owns a small spread over to the east but, according to what folks say, that ain't his chief business."

"What is his chief business?" Slade asked.

The keeper shrugged. "Reckon, according to what folks say, smuggling gets him most of the dinero he throws around mighty free, though there's some that will tell you, when he isn't around, that a little harmless cow-thieving and stage-robbing ain't passed up when a chance comes along. Couldn't say as to that and wouldn't if I could. Folks who talk too free about Graves and what he does is liable to be found up some dark alley comfortably waiting for the undertaker, or so it's said."

"Pancho Graves," Slade repeated. "Odd name combination."

"Uh-huh," agreed the keeper. "Understand the Mexicans he buys goods from that don't pay no duty call him that. Pancho is Mexican talk for Frank, you know. Reckon Frank Graves is his real handle, or the one he uses just now. I've a notion he don't hanker over much to be called Pancho. The story goes that there was a Mexican outlaw not long ago that was called just Pancho. Haven't heard anything of him for a couple of years, but he used to raise heck along both sides of the Border."

Outside sounded another clatter of hoofs. The stable keeper craned his neck toward a window.

"Here comes Graves now, and his chief sidekick, Blaine Gulden!" he exclaimed. "Huh! Gulden's got his head tied up. Wonder how come? Anybody who busted that fire-eyed hellion's knob must be all set to be planted about now!"

Glancing out the window, Slade saw two men riding slowly up the street from the direction of the desert. One was squat, powerfully built with long, dangling arms and an amazing breadth of shoulder. He had dead black eyes, and a mop of curly black hair showing beneath the pushed back brim of his hat. His companion was close to six feet in height but also powerfully built, with a hard mouth and flashing blue eyes. He was clean shaven but the hardness and darkness of his cheeks bespoke a heavy and very dark beard should it be allowed to grow. His hair was black and worn rather long. The brim of his hat was also pushed back and disclosed a bandage swathing his well-shaped head.

The two men rode past without a glance at the stable. Slade followed them with his eyes, the concentration furrow deepening between his black brows. He had instantly recognized Pancho Graves from the description given him by Captain McNelty, but although he could not recall ever seeing the other man before, there was something vaguely familiar about his darkly handsome face and glittering eyes.

Slade cudgeled his brains in an effort to uncover some clue as to where he might have seen Blaine Gulden before, but none came and he concluded Gulden must merely resemble somebody he had once encountered. Anyhow, Graves was the man in whom he was interested. Pancho Graves, pretty definitely established as a smuggler of duty "free" goods back and forth across the Mexican Border, although he had so far never been caught, and now suspected by Captain McNelty of the much more serious offense of dealing in contraband arms destined for troublemakers south of the Rio Grande. The man he, Slade, had been dispatched to Coffin to get something on.

Leaving the stable, Slade had no difficulty locating the eating house which proved to be small but spotlessly clean and with a cheerful air that was enhanced by the smile which wreathed the wrinkled countenance of the old Mexican who was the proprietor.

"Manuel, isn't it?" Slade asked, smiling in turn.

"*Si*, tall *Señor*, so I am called," the other admitted. "The *señor* hungers? Good! I like the one who hungers, for such a one does full justice to the food in which I take pride."

"Then, Manuel, you've sure run into the right hombre," Slade chuckled. "Before I got to town last night I was thinking of slicing a steak off my *caballo's* rump and eating it raw."

Manuel instantly caught the use of the Spanish word for horse, and noted that it was properly pronounced.

"You speak the tongue of my people, *si?*" he asked in Spanish.

"Indifferently well," Slade replied, with a smile, in the same language.

Old Manuel chuckled delightedly. "Before dining, you will share the rare wine with me?" he invited.

"With pleasure," Slade accepted.

The restaurant boasted a tiny bar near and parallel to the door. Manuel shuffled behind it and carefully selected a bottle which he held to the light to show the rich red of its contents. He was about to fill glasses when a waiter, apparently even older than himself, shambled from the kitchen bearing a large bowl of steaming chili for another customer

52

who sat at a far table. As he passed the bar, his hand shook a little and some of the hot and greasy contents of the bowl slopped over onto the floor. Manuel clucked disapprovingly.

"Your pardon, *Patron*," the waiter said humbly and after placing the bowl before the occupant of the table hurried to the kitchen for a mop.

Before he had time to procure the necessary tool and return, the door opened and a big heavy-set man entered. He had warm brown eyes and tawny hair liberally sprinkled with gray. His rugged face was deeply lined and he was undoubtedly far from young. But from the swing of his stride and the spring of his step, it was clear that he had not yet lost the fire and activity of his youth.

That long swinging stride proved his undoing. His forward reaching foot came down on the greasy spot made by the puddle of spilled chili and slipped. He tried to recover, throwing the other foot to the front, but it, too, slipped and he plunged forward in a bone-breaking fall.

Walt Slade left the bar in a ripple of motion. He caught the man's hurtling body, reeled back a step from the impact against his own chest but recovered his balance and saved the other from striking the floor.

The man gripped Slade's arms and straightened up, breathing a bit heavily.

"Son, much obliged," he said. "If it hadn't been for you I'd have busted my neck sure as the devil."

"I doubt if it would have been that bad, sir," Slade replied, rubbing his bruised chest, "but you might have injured an arm."

The other shook his head doubtfully. Old Manuel wiped a suddenly moist brow with a shaking hand.

"*Sangre de Dios, Don Tomaso!*" he exclaimed. "I feared you would suffer the hurt *muy malo!* That such a thing should occur in my *cantina!* You will have the good wine to steady the nerve?"

"Don't mind if I do," the other replied. "Glasses for both of us. Son," he said to Slade, "I'm Tom Ware. I don't believe I caught your handle."

Slade instantly recognized the name as belonging to the man who had made the initial gold strike and who was the owner of the richest mine, the Last Nugget, but he gave no sign; he merely supplied his own name and they shook hands.

"And if you don't mind, we'll sit down at one of the tables to have our wine," Ware said. "That tumble left me just a mite shaky

— not as young as I used to be. I was going to have some breakfast, anyhow."

"I had the same thing in mind, the breakfast part," Slade admitted as they occupied a nearby table. Old Manuel brought the wine and summoned a waiter to take their order for food. Tom Ware sipped his drink and chuckled.

"Thought for a minute I was going to end up in what folks said I'd end up in if I didn't stay out of the Tinto Hills, a coffin," he said. "That's why I named this town Coffin. Named this street, too — *Chaparro,* after a bird."

"The chaparral cock, sometimes called a road runner from its habit of scooting along ahead of a horse or a wagon," Slade interpolated. "How'd you come to name it after old spike-tail, sir?"

"Sort of a funny yarn," Ware replied. "I'd met up with a feller in the desert on my way to the hills. We'd moseyed along together for company's sake for a spell. When we came to the forks of the draw just to the north of here, I gave him his choice. He was going to take the right fork, I'm sure of that. But right then a road runner busted out of the brush and headed up that fork. Feller cussed it plenty and swore he wouldn't follow its trail; 'lowed the darn things always brought him back luck. So he took the other fork, and I took the right one, and located the Last Nugget Mine.

"I've often wondered what became of that feller," he added reflectively. "If he'd come back this way or showed up in town, I've always figured to hand him a slice of the Last Nugget, seeing as he just about *handed* the whole mine to *me* when he chose the left fork of the draw."

"Think you'd know him if you saw him again?" Slade asked casually as the waiter began placing filled dishes before them.

"I've a notion I would," Ware replied. "He was a big fine-looking feller, younger than me, with sharp blue eyes and the blackest and thickest whiskers I ever saw. I know I'd recognize those whiskers if I saw them again. Guess he kept on going when he didn't find anything in the hills, or maybe the Apaches got him. Old Laughing Bear and his bunch were raiding just about then and I wouldn't be surprised if they did get him if he went very far into the hills. I never learned his name. He was close-mouthed about himself and it isn't polite to ask personal questions of a feller you meet casual-like that way, not in this section."

Slade nodded agreement and a period of busy silence followed, as is the way with hungry men when good food is placed before them. Finally Tom Ware pushed back his plate and called for more wine; Slade ordered more coffee.

Ware produced an old black pipe and stuffed it with blacker tobacco; Slade rolled a cigarette. For some time they smoked in comfortable silence, Ware apparently dreamily content, Slade endeavoring to analyze what he had just heard. There was little doubt in his mind but that the man described by Ware was the missing Robert Flint, Edward Duncan's absconding business associate. Ware's story rang true, but he wondered why Duncan, in the course of his investigation, had never heard it. However, the simple explanation quickly offered; Ware, busy with many matters, had never before mentioned his casual meeting with the desert wanderer; or if he had, the incident would have been considered of no account by his hearers and quickly forgotten.

He wondered, too, if Ware would recognize Flint if he chanced to see him without the beard upon which his attention appeared to have concentrated. Quite likely, Slade thought, Ware would meet a clean-shaven Flint on the street and pass him by without a second glance.

Not that he was liable to meet Flint anywhere. Like Ware, Slade was inclined to believe that Flint had met with Indian trouble back in the hills and never got out of them alive. Well, the business was of secondary importance at the moment. The man he desired to learn more about was not Robert Flint but Pancho Graves. He decided to sound out Ware a little.

"I observed a rather remarkable individual riding into town this morning," he remarked idly. "The stable keeper who directed me to this restaurant said he was called Pancho Graves. There was another man with him who also appeared a bit out of the ordinary, Blaine Gulden, I believe the keeper mentioned as his name. Are they connected with the mines?"

Tom Ware's face darkened and he bit hard on his pipe stem. "They're not," he said shortly, "nor with anything else that requires honest work. They're a pair of ornery smugglers, if not worse."

Slade nodded and looked contemplative. "Seems to me I heard something about Graves over to Patricio before I headed this way," he remarked reminiscently. "Sort of call to mind somebody allowing that a fellow named Graves had a lot to do with the running of this section."

"He doesn't," Ware returned, even more shortly. "He's just a hatchet man for Cole Young."

"Cole Young?" Slade repeated interrogatively.

"That's right," said Ware. "Young owns the Square Deal saloon here, the biggest and the worst in town. Managed to get a finger in the political pie of the county. Got a rapscallion named John Blount elected sheriff and somehow pulled wires over to the state capital and elsewhere and got the county seat moved to Coffin. Pancho Graves is just a not-too-bright owlhoot with plenty of guts and a quick trigger finger. That sidekick of his you saw, Gulden, is smarter and I expect even ornrier than Graves, because he *is* smarter; but Cole Young's got brains and knows how to use them. I've no use for Young — I consider him a scalawag of the first order, but I don't underestimate him. He's the man who has more to say as to how Tinto County is run than anybody else and he's been busy ruining this fine town. I don't know what's going to happen the next councilmanic election but I'm mighty scared Young is going to tighten his grip on things. I'm doing all I can to prevent that happening, but I'm no politician and when it comes to that game Young is always two jumps ahead of me. A darn shame, too. I worked hard to make this a prosperous and respectable community for decent folks to live in and be happy and it hurts to see it all spoiled by characters like Young and Graves and Blaine Gulden. Don't know what I can do about it, though," he concluded with a heavy sigh.

"I've a notion maybe things will work out right before the last brand's run," Slade comforted the distraught old man. Ware shot him a peculiar look.

"Son," he said, "I don't know a darn thing about you, where you come from or where you're heading for, but somehow the way you said that makes me feel better."

Ware fixed his gaze on the Ranger. "Son, are you just passing through or do you aim to coil your twine here for a spell?" he asked.

"Well, I've just had a long and hard ride and I plan to loaf around for a few days," Slade replied. "Then if I can tie onto a job of riding or something like that, I may stay in the section for a while. Not a good time of year to be chuck-line riding, so a steady job would be okay. Man has to eat, you know."

"Uh-huh, I know," Ware chuckled. "Many's the time I've filled my belly with wind pudding and nothing else, and that

60

ain't over nourishing. So if you decide to stick around, drop in at my office at the stamp mill and we'll have a little gab. Wouldn't be surprised if I can throw something your way. Sort of owe it to you for saving me from bustin' my awkward neck. Besides," he added, "I've sort of took to you, son. I usually either like folks in a hurry or don't like 'em at all, and you're easy to cotton to on first acquaintance."

"Thank you, sir, I appreciate that," Slade smiled. "Chances are I'll drop in on you before long. Also," he concluded, "I've a notion you like most folks."

Tom Ware smiled in return. "Well," he admitted, "I've usually found that there are more good folks than bad. We don't hear much about the good ones — sort of take them as a matter of course — which to my mind proves there are a lot more good ones than bad ones. It's the bad ones that get talked about, because they're out of the ordinary, and it's the out of the ordinary that starts folks gabbin'. So many good folks that nobody pays them much mind."

Slade nodded agreement to the mine owner's homely philosophy; his experience with people had been somewhat similar. A thought struck him and he asked another casual question.

"From where do you get your supplies — tools, explosives, etc.? This morning when I was walking over from the stable I noticed a road swerving around the base of the hills over to the northeast with wagons traveling it toward town. Is there another town over there?"

"That's right," replied Ware. "Clarksburg, the railroad town, about thirty miles off. Wagon trains and a stage line between here and Clarksburg. Wouldn't be surprised if the railroad builds down here before long; talk about it. Loading pens at Clarksburg for the spreads over to the east. Everything we use comes from Clarksburg by way of that wagon road. The soldiers have a post over there. That's where they started from to round up old Laughing Bear and his Apaches. Not much for them to do nowadays with the Indians corraled on the reservation. Wouldn't be surprised if it's closed before long, like lots of those old military posts. Don't need 'em any more with the Rangers handling all the trouble that busts loose."

"And you never get supplies from down to the southwest? I noted a pack train down that way last night; didn't seem headed this way but I couldn't be sure."

"Heck, no!" grunted Ware. "Nothing

comes from down there except owlhoots like the Graves gang. No settlement within fifty miles."

"Trail down there?"

"Uh-huh, one runs from the lower edge of town through the Mexican settlement, but nobody ever uses it except some of the Mexican mine workers now and then going back to *manana* land for a visit with their folks; them and the owlhoots. You have to know your way through the badlands or you're liable to stay there, what the buzzards leave of you."

Slade nodded, his eyes thoughtful. As he had surmised, to all appearances the loads of dynamite and tools did not come from Coffin. But where did they come from and where in blazes were they headed for, and why! He gave it up for the moment.

Tom Ware drew out a big silver watch and glanced at it. "Have to be getting up to the mill," he announced. "Don't forget to drop in on me, son; you'll always be welcome, and if I don't happen to be at the mill, I'll be at the mine, a mile up the draw and to the right, just past where the left fork cuts off to the west."

He smiled and nodded, paused a moment at the bar to say a few low-voiced words to old Manuel and left the restaurant. Slade finished his smoke and pinched out the butt. He got up and walked to the bar.

"Okay, Manuel, what do I owe you?" he asked.

The old Mexican wrinkled a smile. "Nothing, tall *Señor,*" he said. "Your bill is paid. And *Don Tomaso* says you are to be his guest here for as long as you remain in town."

"Well, that's certainly nice of him," Slade acknowledged, "but I don't see why he should do it."

"*Señor,* by your thought and action so fast you undoubtedly saved *Don Tomaso* from injury most grave," the Mexican replied. "He is a man of appreciation and I beg of you not to refuse his bounty. Do so and he will feel the hurt. He is a man of much money and loves to spend it to bring happiness to others. A fine man, a wonderful man. And I am grateful also, *Señor.* My heart would have been broken in the two pieces had *Don Tomaso* suffered the injury in my *cantina.* With me, tall *Señor,* you must have the last glass of the fine wine."

"*Gracias,*" Slade accepted, "but make this one small, Manuel."

They finished the wine and Slade left the eating house feeling that he had gotten an exceedingly lucky break. He had learned what might have taken him days of probing around to uncover. It appeared, among other things, that Captain McNelty had been misinformed as to who was the real head of the turbulent factions in Coffin and Tinto County. If Tom Ware said Cole Young and not Pancho Graves was the big he-wolf, Slade believed that very likely he was. Just where Young stood in the arms smuggling across the Rio Grande of which Pancho Graves was suspected remained to be determined. At any rate, Slade decided to get a look at Young.

CHAPTER 5

Meanwhile, an angry discussion was going on in the back room of Cole Young's saloon. Young was there, his one eye gleaming, his scarred face more bad tempered than usual, and burly Pancho Graves and saturnine Blaine Gulden, with several hard-looking characters who stood back and took no part in the argument.

"If we hadn't been pretty well scattered when that slug hit the dynamite box, like as not we'd have all been killed instead of just two of the boys being cashed in and a few more with lead punctures or banged up by flying rocks," Graves declared. "The pack horses were scattered, too, so we just lost a couple of boxes of powder instead of the whole cargo."

"It was a fool thing to do, picking a row that way with a wandering cowhand," said Young. "If you'd just let him ride past he'd very likely have not noticed anything out of the ordinary; pack trains are not unusual in this section."

"How were we to know what he was?" retorted Graves. "The boys were jumpy anyhow; there's been soldiers snooping around in the badlands of late. Say they're on the lookout for some Apaches that slipped away from the reservation, but that sounds like a phony yarn to me. They may have caught on to something. Anyhow, somebody pulled trigger when he showed up all of a sudden outa the dark, and the rest of us joined in to make a finish job of it. But that infernal horse he rode was dancing and weaving and sliding like a hen on a hot skillet, and he went through us like a greased pig."

"Didn't anybody see him well enough to tell what he looked like?" asked Young.

"I saw him, and felt him," said Blaine Gulden as he gingerly fingered his bandaged head. "He was mighty tall and mighty broad. I didn't get much of a look at his face before his gun barrel landed on my head, but I'd say he had a hawk nose."

"Not much of a description," grunted Young, "but he's likely to show up here in town and maybe one of you will recognize him. He should be taken care of before he gets too much chance to talk."

"You're right about that," agreed Graves. "Well, anyhow, we got enough of the stuff through to take care of the chore whenever you say the word."

"I haven't the word to say," Young replied. "All we can do for the present is sit tight and let things work out, which, unless my calculations are wrong, and I don't think they are, will be soon. In fact, I'll be just as pleased if they do hold back a bit after what happened last night, until it blows over. If that cowhand, or whoever the devil he was, blabs about it before we get a chance to shut him up, somebody might figure things out, now or later."

"Not likely," said Gulden.

"Maybe no," Young conceded, "but we're playing for big stakes and we don't want to lose because of some fool slip. Just keep your mouths shut and your eyes open for a few days, and if you spot that hellion, get rid of him. I won't feel right so long as he's running around loose. Let him start talking in the wrong quarters and somebody may get to thinking, and we don't want that."

Pancho Graves' florid face wrinkled in querulous lines. "I can't keep from feeling bothered about this complicated scheme you've figured out, Young," he complained. "Too darn many angles to suit me. And we've been doing all right as it was. Plenty of cows slid south, and the next gun shipment is all set to go when you give the word. Yes, we've been doing all right."

"Peanuts!" scoffed Young. "What I've worked up will end having us all sitting pretty for life."

"If there ain't a slip somewhere," Graves grumbled morosely.

"About that hellion we had the brush with last night," observed the glitter-eyed Gulden. "He's my meat. I owe him something for this busted head."

"From what you said of him, I figure you'd better watch your step if you do run into him," Young observed dryly. "Sounds like bad medicine to me."

"Next time maybe it won't be dark and pack horses skalleyhooting every which way," Gulden replied grimly. "I'll take care of him."

"Hope so," said Young. "Well, let's go out and have a drink. I believe everything is taken care of. I sent word to Blount to drop around."

The other offered no objection and the unsavory bunch trooped into the saloon and lined up at the rear end of the bar. Men nearby, some of them hard-looking individuals themselves, respectfully made way for the Graves bunch.

Walt Slade sauntered back to the livery stable to make sure all Shadow's wants were cared for, then departed to look over the town. It was a busy and bustling place and everybody appeared cheerful and prosperous. The air quivered to the incessant pound and grumble of the stamps, huge steel pestles heavily shod with iron that pulverized the gold ore into a water paste from which the precious metal was separated by the amalgam process. The mills were big ones, eight-stamp affairs driven by steam and of the most modern equipment; evidently Tom Ware and his associates went in for only the best. Down a road that curved around to the northeast into the hills, came streams of huge wagons, each drawn by six mules, that bore the gold ore from the mines to the mills.

Slade paused and gazed up the draw. Coffin was bathed in sunshine but to the north a tremendous thunderhead palpitated, like a great tree with black blossoms, and slowly climbed the long slant of the sky. It's baleful shadow spread over the hills and they seemed to glower. Slowly, steadily that ominous shadow crept toward the town on the rattlesnake's jaw, slowly, steadily, heavy with evil, or so it seemed to the tall Ranger. He laughed at his over-active imagination and strolled on, pausing to glance in windows, noting faces that drifted past, gradually working toward the east end of the town. He paused before a solidly constructed building across the plate glass windows of which was a legend that proclaimed it Cole Young's Square Deal saloon.

For a moment Slade hesitated, then he pushed through the swinging doors and entered, his all-embracing glance sweeping the big room.

At this early hour there were not many people in the saloon, but a group at the far end of the bar instantly attracted Slade's attention. He recognized one of the group as Pancho Graves, another was Blaine Gulden. It was not hard to spot Cole Young, a powerfully-built man slightly under six feet with one empty eye socket and a badly scarred face. His hair was grizzled, more gray than black, but despite his disfigured countenance, Slade thought his face looked considerably younger than his graying black hair seemed to indicate. Prematurely gray, Slade felt. He also sensed that Cole Young had once been a handsome man, but with one lid lying flat on the empty socket, part of the bridge of his nose gone, one cheekbone smashed in and his mouth twisted sideways by still another puckered cicatrix, he was not very pleasant to look at. It was horribly apparent that the poor devil must have been desperately wounded at one time or another. A wonder he had survived such appalling injuries.

All this Slade noted in one swift glance as he sauntered to the bar and ordered a drink. Heads had turned quickly when he entered but there was nothing unusual about that in a place with the reputation the Square Deal enjoyed.

After those first swift glances of appraisal, however, he was ignored by the occupants of the far end of the bar who were talking together. He did not hear Blaine Gulden en's excited whisper, "Boys, that's him! That's the hellion I was telling you about. I'll swear to it."

"Holy hoppin' horntoads!" Pancho Graves exclaimed hoarsely, his voice barely audible. "Blaine, are you sure?"

"Yes, I'm sure," Gulden replied. "What's the matter with you?"

"If this don't beat the devil and all his helpers!" sputtered Graves. "Of all the hellions in Texas it would have to be *him!*"

"You know him?" asked Young.

"Yes, I know him," Graves answered. "I saw him once, over at Proctor, when he killed Doc Skelton and Nate Richardson, two salty gents who were almighty good with a gun but not quite good enough. That's El Halcon!"

Blaine Gulden gave a low whistle but Cole Young did not appear particularly impressed.

"And who's El Halcon?" he asked. "I never heard of him."

"He's the smartest and saltiest owlhoot in Texas or points west," said Graves. "Ain't never been caught at anything though there's plenty against him. No sheriff has been able to *prove* a thing against him. Got killings to his credit but 'pears all the gents he cashed in were pretty ornery specimens, too, and he always got away with it."

"I never saw him before, but I heard about him, over at Tombstone, Arizona," said Gulden. "It was said he backed down Curly Bill Brocius and John Ringo and even stood up to Wyatt Earp and Doc Holliday, or so I was told. Plumb pizen with a gun, and you'll notice he packs two. Last night I'd have swore he was shooting with five or six all at once."

"Well, what of it?" asked Young. "Plenty of quick-draw men with slow brains."

"Nothing slow about El Halcon's brains, as you're liable to find out if something isn't done in a hurry," said Pancho Graves.

"What do you mean by that?" demanded Young.

"I mean," Graves said slowly and significantly, "that his specialty is horning in on good things other folks have started and skimming off the cream. He always seems to find out what's building up and gets in on the ground floor to cut himself a nice slice. The gents who start things end with their toes up and El Halcon rides off with stuffed pouches. Understand what I mean?"

"Yes, I understand what you're driving at," Young conceded, "but I'm not particularly bothered by any brush-popping outlaw who rides into town."

"All right," said Graves, "but I wouldn't be a bit surprised if he figures out what we intended to do with that dynamite."

"You're loco!" scoffed Young.

"Maybe I am," Graves admitted, "but I *am* bothered. Up to now I've just been an honest smuggler with a little sashayin' sideline now and then and the El Halcon sort don't pay any mind to such chicken feed. But this thing we're working on is right down his alley."

"But if everybody knows he's an owlhoot, why not have the sheriff lock him up?" suggested one of Graves' henchmen who hitherto had not spoken.

"On what charges?" snorted Graves. "Didn't I tell you nobody has ever been able to get anything on him? He'd make a plumb fool of fat Johnny Blount, and even if Blount did manage to lock him up, he couldn't keep him locked up with nothing against him. Don't forget, Hilary Vane is still the judge and Vane would turn him loose pronto when Blount couldn't bring forward any evidence against him. We own the sheriff's office, but we don't own Hilary Vane, and we're not likely to. All we'd do is just tip our hand. El Halcon would figure mighty fast who was back of the move and would know we're scared of him and would begin wondering why. Then he'd proceed to find out why."

"Guess the only thing is to do away with him," said Gulden.

"Uh-huh, but that's considerable of a chore," said Graves. "If you're tired of living, go ahead and pick a row with him and force him to draw. You'll be dead before you clear leather. Oh, I know you're good, and so am I, and Young's maybe better'n either one of us, but even Young ain't got no business going up against El Halcon."

"It's plain to see that it will require brains to deal with the gentleman," observed Cole Young. "So I'll take over the chore of eliminating him. There are things other than fast gun hands."

"You're welcome," grunted Graves, "but you'd better be mighty spry, and smart as a treeful of owls. Anyhow, we don't have to worry over what happened last night being talked about; El Halcon don't talk."

"Very comforting, after what you've been telling me of him," Young remarked sarcastically. He turned to a wiry little man with beady black eyes, lank black hair and a dark, expressionless face.

"Pete," he said, "you're pretty good at tracking folks through the brush, or out of it. I want you to keep on that big devil's tail. Find out where he's staying, and anything else you can learn about him, where he goes, what he does, who he talks with."

"And if I can, I keel?" Pete asked softly, his thin lips barely moving.

"Yes," Young acceded, "if you can; but try and not get yourself killed — first."

Blaine Gulden's finely shaped mouth twitched slightly, but if Pete also caught the innuendo he did not show it.

"Now all of you get out of here," Young ordered, "and come back after dark."

CHAPTER 6

Unaware that he was the subject under discussion, Walt Slade studied the group in the back-bar mirror. The vague feeling persisted that he had seen Blaine Gulden's gloomily handsome face somewhere, but for the life of him he could not recall when, where or under what circumstances.

While he was pondering the matter, the gathering at the end of the bar broke up. All save Cole Young headed for the door, passing Slade without a glance in his direction. A little later Young came strolling up on the far side of the bar and paused before Slade. His twisted smile revealed teeth as white and even as El Halcon's own.

"Stranger hereabouts?" he asked affably. Slade nodded.

"Always glad to have a stranger come into my establishment," Young said. "If he comes in once, he'll come in again. That name on the window means just what it says; in here you get a square deal. It pays off."

"Square dealing always pays off in the long run," Slade agreed.

"My sentiments," said Young. "When a man comes in here I don't care who he is or what he's done, I treat him right. And I've found that if you treat folks right, they'll usually treat you right. Take those boys who just left — they may run a few wet cows across the Rio Grande now and then or slip some stuff past the Customs people, but I feel that's no concern of mine. They come in, have some drinks, play a few hands of cards or have a whirl or two on the dance floor and behave like gentlemen while they're in here. That's all I ask. Some folks condemn me for talking with them, but why shouldn't I? If they have broken the law, that's a matter for the proper law-enforcement officers. I have certain rules of behavior in here and I see to it that they are obeyed. What's done outside my door is certainly not in my province."

Slade listened gravely to the saloonkeeper's ruminations on the relationship of the dealer and customer but with considerable inner amusement. He knew perfectly well that Cole Young's delineation of his trade philosophy was a subtle endeavor to draw him out, something difficult to do when Walt Slade did not wish to be drawn out.

"Quite logical, from your viewpoint and doubtless subscribed to by — others," he said.

Cole Young looked a bit bewildered. "I make it a practice not to stick my nose into other people's affairs," he said.

"Laudatory, for one in your position," Slade commented.

This time a baffled expression crossed Young's disfigured countenance and his one eye seemed to gleam more brightly. He drew a deep breath, hesitated, ended by beckoning the nearest bartender.

"My private bottle," he directed. He smiled again, his white-toothed, twisted smile.

"One on the house," he said, "the very best in stock," and filled Slade's glass to the brim.

Slade's respect for Cole Young rose. A man who can admit defeat with a grin is a man to be reckoned with. "Got some chores to attend to," Young said. "Hope you'll see fit to drop in again." With a nod he passed to the end of the bar, opened a door and closed it behind him.

But as he finished his drink and sauntered out, Slade wondered a bit uneasily if Young had altogether suffered defeat. If he was as shrewd as Slade gave him credit for being, he had very likely established one thing in his own mind to his own satisfaction: that the man with whom he had sparred conversationally was something other than a chuck-line riding cowhand of the common garden variety. Which was possibily just what Young wanted to find out. Why? Slade didn't know. Perhaps just the natural interest in a stranger entering his establishment, but considering what old Tom Ware had said, added to Young's association with Pancho Graves, Slade was not so sure. Well, whatever it was it could bide. Slade shrugged broad shoulders and pushed open the swinging doors.

When he stepped into the street, Slade saw that the shadow of the great cloud had crept forward until it shrouded Coffin in gloom. But to the north the edge of the cloud was lifting from the horizon to show a widening streak of sunny blue sky. A good omen? Meaning that trouble was coming to Coffin but would pass? Slade chuckled at the manifestly absurd conceit and dismissed it from his mind.

Slade had arisen early and it still lacked more than an hour of noon; there were many hours of daylight still ahead. Gazing up the wide draw that bored into the northern hills, he arrived at an impulsive decision. He did not see that there was anything he could do about Pancho Graves at the moment, for he still did not know just where or how to begin his investigation of the smuggler's activities, and his curiosity as to the fate of the missing embezzler, Robert Flint, had been fanned by his conversation with Tom Ware. He returned to the stable and got the rig on Shadow.

"May be just a darn fool ramble," he told the horse, "but we're going to take a little prowl up that oversized ditch and see where it leads to. Very likely just a waste of time, for it's reasonable to believe that prospectors have combed it from end to end since the big gold strike down here. Just the same, we're going to have a look-see."

Shadow, who appeared to be well rested and showed no ill effects from the long trip across the desert, offered no objections, so they set out. Slade paused at a general store to replenish the supply of staple provisions he always kept in his saddle pouches, for he never knew how long he might be on the trail, and a man must eat.

Slade rode north to the forks of the draw. He pulled up for a moment and gazed up the right branch, from which the ore wagons streamed. Up there, less than a mile, he had gathered from Tom Ware, was the tunnel of the Last Nugget Mine. Farther on were the tunnels and shafts of the other mines opened up after Young's discovery. He did not turn right, however, but into the left fork that quickly developed a slight westerly trend. He was really of the opinion that he was riding on a fool's errand. Surely prospectors had long ago gone over every inch of the draw.

For several miles he did encounter evidence of exhaustive prospecting, but before long the signs of pick and hammer and drill ceased, the reason quickly apparent to Slade.

Shortly before the untimely death of his father following business reversals that resulted in the loss of the elder Slade's ranch, Walt Slade had graduated from a college of engineering. His plan had been to take a postgraduate course in special subjects to round out his education. This became impossible for the time being and when Captain Jim McNelty, his father's friend, with whom young Walt had worked some during summer vacations, suggested that he come into the Rangers for a while and study in his spare time, Slade thought the idea a good one. That was some years before and long since he had acquired all and more from private study than he could have hoped to get from the postgrad. He was ready to be an engineer, and intended to become one, later. But Ranger work had gotten a strong hold on him and he was loath to sever connections with the famous corps of law-enforcement officers. Plenty of time to be an engineer; he'd stick with the Rangers for a while.

So Walt Slade surveyed his surroundings with the eye of a geologist, and the story they told was as easy for him to read as the printed page. Small wonder the experienced prospectors had abandoned their search for metal-bearing ledges and had never gone far beyond this point.

The rock formation of the draw had changed, doubtless due to a slip, a subsidence or an upheaval in the course of some convulsion of nature in ages gone. The quartz cliffs were replaced by traprock and limestone, with limestone predominating. In neither of these petrological outcroppings would precious metal be found.

"Well, this changes the outlook," Slade said to Shadow. "If Flint did happen to perish in the hills there's a chance we may find some evidence of the fact. Bones don't disappear in five years, and the smoke stains left on rocks at camping spots remain a long time, especially in a dry country like this one. Incidentally, Apaches made a practice of striking at camping spots, especially early in the morning when the campers are just getting up. The dark hours are sacred to ancestral gods, so the Indians would creep up and surround a camp at night and strike as dawn was breaking. Let's go, horse, and see what we can find out."

It was not until the day was growing to a close and the shadows were already curdling in the hollows did the search bear fruit. Far up the wash, on the third of a series of broad benches, where a spring trickled from beneath an overhanging cliff, Slade found bones.

But they were not the bones of a man; a single glance sufficed to show that. They were the bones of a burro. A second, more searching glance revealed the cause of the little animal's death. There was a round hole in the skull just between the empty eye sockets.

Slade dismounted in order to search the tall grass more carefully. He had taken but a couple of steps when he halted abruptly. Nearly hidden by the fading grass were more bones — the skeleton of a man.

There were few coyotes in these hills and

the buzzards had gotten to the body first and stripped it of flesh, so the skeleton was very nearly intact. A smashed rib on the left side showed where a bullet had taken effect.

"Got him dead center, poor devil," Slade remarked to Shadow. "Well, begins to look like this is all that's left of Robert Flint. Mr. Duncan will be glad to learn of it, as it tends to settle his problem. That is, if we can turn up something that will provide corroborative evidence that these are the bones of Flint."

With this in mind he began a careful search of the surroundings. Very quickly he discovered the iron head of a heavy miner's pick, the wooden handle quite rotted away. Then a steel drill and a chipping hammer. All but disintegrated shreds of fabric and rope scattered near the burro's bones were the remains of the pack. Yes, all signs pointed to Robert Flint as the victim of an Apache raid. Slade estimated that the spot just about terminated the distance Flint would have been expected to cover after parting with Tom Ware. Apparently the Indians got him the first night.

But a little later the Ranger made a discovery that puzzled him. The underside of the overhanging cliff was blackened in several places, denoting that more than one fire had been kindled. The prospector would hardly have lit more than one at a time, and the raiding Apaches certainly wouldn't have paused for that purpose. Nor could Slade see any reason why Flint would have picked this as a camping spot for several days. But there was no doubt but a number of fires had been kindled, for where wind and rain could not reach them, he found ashes mixed with the soft earth. Shaking his head, he went back to where the skeleton lay, rolled a cigarette and stood regarding the sad remains of what once had been a man.

Suddenly he leaned forward, the concentration furrow deepening between his brows, his forgotten cigarette burning toward his fingers. He stooped, gently lifted the skull from its resting place. It had become detached from the vertebrae and lay a little to one side. Pinching out the cigarette, he turned the skull over and over in his hands, studying it from all angles, and as he did so, his eyes began to glow.

"Shadow," he said to the black horse, who was contentedly grazing nearby, "Shadow, I'm getting a notion. I think I'm right about this thing, but I'm going to make sure; I'm going to send it to somebody who will *know*. If I am right, and I believe I am, it will open up a new and interesting angle to this business."

Securing a spare neckerchief from his saddle pouch, he carefully wrapped the skull and stored it in the pouch. Then he began an exhaustive exploration of the surrounding terrain, quartering the ground with the greatest of care, gradually working to the east end of the brush-grown bench, finding no more bones and nothing else of interest. Finally he turned, heavy with thought, and retraced his steps to where Shadow stood. As he drew near he noticed that the big horse was blowing softly through his nose, his ears pricked forward, his gaze on a belt of thicket about a dozen yards to the west.

CHAPTER 7

Slade's own glance shifted to the thicket. He heard a slight rustling of the leaves, saw a flicker of movement and hurled himself sideways and down even as the hidden gun cracked and a bullet yelled through the space his body had occupied an instant before. Rolling over and over, slugs spatting the ground all around him, he reached the dubious shelter of a fairly long but low boulder and flattened out behind it. Cautiously he raised his head until the high crown of his hat just peeped above the top of the rock. Instantly a slug tore through it.

"Good shooting!" he muttered as he flattened out again and drew his guns. With a swift move he thrust one over the lip of the boulder and fired two shots. An answering bullet chipped a fragment from the rock and yelled off into space. He knew by the heaviness of the reports that the drygulcher was using a rifle and wished for his own Winchester, but it was snugged in the saddle boot out of reach. Every sense tensely alert, he considered the situation.

He was on an uncomfortably hot spot. Right now he had the drygulcher pretty well stymied, but that satisfactory condition would not obtain for long. It was getting dark fast and soon the hellion would be able to slide around through the growth undetected and gain a point where he could get in a killing shot. Something had to be done, and in a hurry.

Slade ejected the two spent shells from his gun and replaced them with fresh cartridges. He waited a moment or two for the gloom to deepen, then balanced his hat on the end of one gun barrel. He raised it slowly and cautiously to simulate a man peering over the boulder. The rifle boomed and the hat went sailing through the air.

But this time Slade saw the orange flash in the thickening murk under the brush. Both his guns let go with a rattling crash as he raked the growth back and forth with a hail of lead, counting his shots. At the ninth he paused, thumbs hooked over the cocked hammers of his Colts.

From the thicket came a scream that crescendoed to a bubbling shriek and ended in an eerie whistling accompanied by a queer staccato thudding as of foot heels beating a tattoo on the hard ground.

The sound ceased as abruptly as it had begun and utter silence followed. Slade crouched tense and waiting, his guns ready for instant action, straining eyes and ears.

But the silence remained unbroken. Shadow, who had been snorting and blowing, gazed toward the thicket a moment, then dropped his head and resumed his interrupted grazing.

"Looks like I got him, and I don't think a second one's holed up there," Slade muttered. He waited another minute or two, then surged to his feet and darted forward through the almost full dark, weaving and ducking, until he reached the edge of the growth.

Nothing happened. For an instant he poised behind the leafy screen, then parted the branches and peered through them. He could barely make out an indistinct shape sprawled on the ground. He reached down, gripped a shirt collar and hauled the body of the drygulcher into the last dying light.

He proved to be a scrawny little man with lank black hair. His glazed eyes appeared also to be black, but Slade could not be sure in that light.

Where had he seen that lean, dark face before? In a flash of recognition he recalled that the man had been one of the group gathered about Pancho Graves and Blaine Gulden in Cole Young's saloon. He straightened up and his lips pursed in a whistle.

"Shadow," he said, "the devils work fast. They must have caught onto something or suspect something, just what I don't know. Thanks, feller, for tipping me off to that sidewinder. Otherwise I'd very likely have walked into the hot end of a slug. This is getting plumb interesting. Well, guess I'd better get a fire going and cook something to eat. Don't think there'll be any more excitement tonight. Then we'll give this hellion a more careful once-over."

He got the rig off the black horse so that it could graze in comfort and kindled a fire in the shadow of the overhang. He abruptly remembered that which, busy with his thoughts, he had forgotten; the fellow must have had a horse. He searched the thicket and after a bit found the cayuse, tied to a branch some distance back along the bench in the direction of Coffin. It was a good looking animal wearing a Mexican brand that meant nothing to Slade. He removed the rig and turned the horse loose to graze, which it immediately started doing. Slade bestowed a pat on it and went back to his fire. Soon he had coffee bubbling in a little flat bucket and bacon and eggs sizzling in a small skillet. He ate his simple meal by the light of the fire and the silvery glow of the half moon. Then he smoked a leisurely cigarette and turned his attention to the corpse that lay just inside the ring of fire light. A search of the fellow's pockets revealed nothing of interest aside from plenty of money; evidently he had been doing quite well by himself. Slade wondered if some of the gold double-eagles represented the price of murder with himself as the intended victim. His belt gun was a regulation Forty-five that showed signs of long usage and the rest of his equipment were of the ordinary rangeland variety. Slade found his rifle lying just inside the fringe of the thicket. It was a good Winchester with nothing to differentiate it from any other of the same date and pattern.

"His sort never packs anything that might tie him up with somebody else," Slade told Shadow. "This time, however, he's definitely tied up — with the Graves gang, at least in my opinion, though Graves and the rest could maintain he was just a barroom acquaintance and not really connected with them in any way. And very likely they'd get away with it. Doesn't matter, anyhow. *I* know now who to look out for, and that's all that counts."

He debated what to do with the body. No sense in packing it to town; nothing would be accomplished by so doing, and another disposal might puzzle and worry the rest of the bunch. With the help of the moonlight Slade searched out a shallow crevice into which he dumped the corpse, on top of it the saddle, bridle and rifle. Then he filled the crevice to the brim with loose stones. With a nod of satisfaction, he went back to his camp, rolled another cigarette and settled down comfortably to digest the affair along with his dinner.

It was painfully evident that the Graves gang was out to get him. Why? The answer was obscure. Perhaps he had been recognized as El Halcon with an owlhoot reputation, or as a Texas Ranger; Slade was inclined to think the former. But why should the smugglers be so anxious to eliminate him, to the extent of having him trailed out of town with cold-blooded murder the objective? As El Halcon he posed no threat to Graves' smuggling activities. That field was wide open and any enterprising brush-popper could get into the business without infringing on another outfit's preserves. The Rangers did not pay much attention to smuggling, which along the Border was regarded by many as legitimate enterprise. Slade knew that many a prosperous and respected Border businessman got his start dealing in goods that paid no duty. The Rangers were taking an interest in Graves only because it had been reported that he had added gun running to his questionable operations. Graves might suspect him of being a Ranger, but the murder of a Texas Ranger was something that caused the boldest outlaw to hesitate. Kill one and another, or several, immediately took his place, and added then to Ranger enforcement of law and order was Ranger vengeance, before the threat of which the most desperate quailed. No, it was much more probable that Graves and his bunch had spotted him as El Halcon. And back came the question, why go to such lengths to remove him from the picture. The only logical answer was that Graves and Company were engaged in something that could be jeopardized by possible activity on his part.

He wondered if there could be some sort of a tie-up with the mysterious cavalcade packing tools and dynamite somewhere from somewhere. From what he had been able to learn of the section and the trails leading to it, he was inclined to believe that the dynamite had by some obscure route been slipped out of Coffin, where there was plenty available. But where the devil was it going and for what purpose? Slade could not remotely imagine an answer to either question.

He fervently hoped that Graves and his bunch had spotted him as El Halcon rather than a Texas Ranger, although that would mean grave danger to himself. A man with an owlhoot reputation was fair game and lawless elements would not hesitate to wipe him out if to do so was to their advantage. But Slade had found the somewhat dubious reputation he enjoyed in some quarters very helpful in his work as a Ranger. Avenues of information were open to him that would be closed to a known peace officer, and opportunities presented because outlaws would take chances with him they would hesitate to risk against a man with all the power and prestige of the Texas Rangers to back him up.

Captain McNelty had more than once protested the risk he ran by doing nothing to refute the opinion of many, including some puzzled sheriffs and other peace officers, that he was an extremely shrewd and capable lone wolf member of the outlaw clan; but the old commander was forced to admit Slade got results by following the course he had mapped out for himself. So Captain Jim grumbled but did not forbid his lieutenant and ace man working under-cover at every opportunity.

Dismissing his problems for the night, Slade spread his blanket beside the dying fire and went to sleep. No need to bother about Laughing Bear and his marauding Apaches; they were either dead or confined to the reservation. And he did not think anybody connected with the Graves gang had followed the trail of the gent who was now sleeping peacefully under a ton or so of boulders.

CHAPTER 8

Dawn found him awake. He cooked some breakfast, gave Shadow a good rubdown and cinched his saddle into place. Then he mounted and rode north by east along the bench. He rode for several miles in an effort to discover if there was a feasible route out of the hills to the northeast and found none that was not fraught with difficulty and danger. The benches criss-crossed in every direction and between the rugged hills were hollows that ran this way and that. He decided it was possible to leave the hills in this direction and that no doubt the dry wash provided the less difficult route, but a little farther on he changed his mind. From a point of elevation he could see that the wide gulch curved to the east and south in a great sweep, apparently doubling back on itself.

"Wouldn't be surprised if we could get back to town by way of this overgrown ditch," he told Shadow, "but I'm pretty sure it would be the longer route, so let's backtrack and head for your stable and a helping of oats. No sense in prowling around up here any longer, at least not yet. If certain things work out the way I figure they should, a little more investigating up here may be in order. Let's go!" He turned the big black and started the trip back to Coffin.

With no need to be on the lookout for camping spots or signs left by a man who had disappeared into the hills five years before, he covered the distance to town in much less time than had been required the day before. It was early afternoon when he reached Coffin. He stabled Shadow, then repaired to a nearby general store where he purchased heavy wrapping paper, twine and a stick of sealing wax. Returning to the stable, he took the neckerchief-wrapped skull from his saddle pouch, along with a sheet of paper and an envelope, and carried them upstairs to his little room over the stalls. There he wrote a short letter which he signed and fastened to one of the parietal bones of the skull with a dab of wax. With the wrapping paper and the twine, he made a neat package of the skull, sealing it with the wax, and addressing it to a Professor of Comparative Anatomy at Baylor University. Descending the stairs, he repaired to the post office a short distance down Chaparro Street.

"Send it first class, there's a letter inside," he directed the postmaster. "There should be an answer in a week or less. I'll call for it."

His next stop was Manuel's little restaurant around the corner. The old Mexican greeted him cordially and set before him the best the house could provide, a bountiful repast, indeed, to which Slade did ample justice.

"*Don Tomaso* he asked about you," said Manuel. "Expressed the hope that you would visit him soon. You should do so, *Señor,* he is the fine man and will be pleased to advance your interests."

Slade promised to visit the mine owner shortly, which he fully intended to do.

Leaving the restaurant, Slade walked back to his room to smoke and think. Later in the evening he made a point of dropping in at the Square Deal. Cole Young, at the far end of the bar, noted his entrance and beckoned Slade to join him.

"Want you to know Sheriff John Blount," he said, indicating a wondrously fat man who stood nearby. "John, this is — come to think of it, feller, I don't believe I got your name the other time you were in here."

Slade supplied it and the sheriff took his hand impressively. His own was very moist.

"Anybody Cole thinks well of is okay in my book," he said in a ridiculously high and squeaking voice, incongruous in one of such bulk.

"John's all right, even if he does hide behind a tin dishpan," said Young. "He doesn't stand for foolishness but doesn't see any sense in interfering with the boys when they're having a good time, even if they do get a bit rowdy now and then."

"Why should I?" squeaked Mr. Blount. "The rock-busters from the mines and the cowhands from the spreads over east have to let off steam every now and then, especially on paydays. So long as they stick to themselves and don't bother other folks, let 'em ruckus a bit, says I."

The sheriff's face was good-humored but rather stupid, Slade thought. His little pale eyes set deep in rolls of flesh, were shifty, his face blue-black where it was shaven and the muscles of his mouth could not quite keep it in place, and he had nicked teeth. Slade was of the opinion that Sheriff Blount was putty in Cole Young's hands, which Tom Ware had maintained he was.

"Told you you'd come back," chuckled Young. "Folks always do, once they've been here."

"No reason I know of why I should not," Slade smiled.

"That's right, that's right," broke in the sheriff. "No reason why a feller wouldn't want to come back to Cole's place — best in town."

Slade did not argue the point. He realized that Cole Young was covertly studying him. He had a feeling that Young was consumed with curiosity over something and didn't know how to go about satisfying it.

"Figure to coil your twine in the section for a while, Mr. Slade?" the sheriff asked.

"I might, if I can tie onto something worth while," Slade replied. "I plan to take it easy for a few days and then I may try to sign up with some outfit. 'Pears to be a nice section."

"It is, it is," declared the sheriff. "None better, none better. Nice folks here. Better stick around a while, Mr. Slade."

After a little more desultory conversation, Slade said good day to Young and the sheriff and left to stroll about the town.

Shortly after Slade's departure, Pancho Graves and Blaine Gulden entered. Gulden looked amused, but Graves was plainly in a very bad temper. His face was flushed and there was a reddish glow in the depths of his dead black eyes.

"Well, I see El Halcon is back in town," Young remarked after they exchanged greetings.

"Yes, and Pete is not back in town," Graves said.

"And what's the answer?" Young asked.

"The answer," Graves retorted angrily, "is that Pete is lying up in the hills somewhere

99

with the buzzards picking his bones."

"Very likely," conceded Young. "What I'd like to know is why did that sidewinder ride into the hills?"

"I don't know," said Graves. "Pete saw him start out and said he was going to tail him. I'd say Pete tried to take a shot at him somewhere and ended up eating lead himself. I tell you that big hellion is plumb pizen!"

"No doubt of that," agreed Young. "You can't trail that kind through the brush without him catching on. If Pete hadn't been a bungling fool he'd never have made a try for him."

"Pete was one of the best trackers that ever came out of Mexico," Graves retorted.

"But not good enough," grinned Blaine Gulden, who appeared to get pleasure from his companions' discomfiture.

"He's plumb pizen," Graves repeated. "What the devil are we going to do about him?"

"Lay off him for a while," counseled Young. "Keep an eye on him but don't make a try for him till a real good opportunity occurs, or we make one. We've got to move cautiously and avoid any more slips. The stakes we're playing for are too big to take chances with."

"For two pesos, I'd throw up the whole business and head west," Graves growled.

"What's the matter, losing your nerve?" sneered Young.

"No, I'm not losing my nerve," Graves replied, "but I've always been able to avoid serious trouble because I understand when I'm up against something dangerous. Why do you think I pulled out of Mexico? I was doing fine down there and had the *rurales* running around in circles. I got word that old *El Presidente* was pulling back his mounted police and sending up a company of regulars from Mexico City, with Yaqui scouts to guide them. I left while the leaving was good."

"I can understand how you felt about that," Young admitted, "but we're not up against a company — just one man."

"But he appears to be the whole blasted army," grumbled Graves. "Oh, well, I suppose we *should* be able to handle him."

"We will be," Young declared confidently. "And anyhow I can't see any cowhand turned outlaw figuring out what we have in mind, or even understanding it. Just sit tight."

CHAPTER 9

Slade loafed about the town until after dark, ate his dinner at Manuel's restaurant and went to bed early. The following morning after breakfast, he rode over to the Last Nugget quartz mill for a visit with Tom Ware.

"Mr. Ware is at the mine office," a clerk told him. "It isn't far, just about a mile up the right fork of the draw. Follow the road and you can't miss it."

Slade thanked the clerk, set out for the mine, passing trains of ore wagons rumbling down to the mill. The tunnel mouth was a scene of bustling activity. Teamsters shouted and swore, ore rattled down the chutes from the bins to thud and clatter in the wagon beds. Steam hissed, hoisting machinery whirred and the pumps clanked steadily. He located the office and was warmly welcomed by Tom Ware.

"How'd you like to have a look at the in-nards of the diggin's?" Ware suggested. "It's old hat to me but I've a notion a cowhand would find it interesting."

Slade smiled slightly and agreed.

"I'll have your critter put in the stable with the other stock," Ware said and whooped for a wrangler who was introduced to

Shadow and the big black permitted him to lead him away.

"One-man horse, eh?" chuckled Ware.

"Try to put a hand on him without a proper instroduction and lose about half of it," Slade replied.

Ware chuckled again. "I like that kind of a horse," he said. "Dependable critters, more so than some men. I like burros, too. You can always depend on them — to kick your slats loose when you're least expecting it. All right, let's go."

They procured cap lights and entered the tunnel, keeping close to the side wall to avoid the loaded ore carts that creaked toward the open air and the empties going in the other direction. After a while they came to a shaft down which they were dropped on a small platform to the lowest level, where men were drilling and digging. Over their heads towered a vast network of interlocking timbers as large as a man's body that held the walls of the gutted lode apart. The framework soared upward so far that no eye could pierce to the summit through the closing gloom. It was like peering up through the clean-picked ribs and bones of some colossal skeleton.

Tom Ware explained things to his companion and Slade listened in silence, not seeing fit to mention that in reality he knew considerably more about the technicalities of the mine than did its owner.

After a long tramp through the resounding dark, they came to the head of the lowest drift, where steam drills chattered, shovels scraped and sledges thudded. Before them was the face of the drift where the drill men were busy boring holes to receive the dynamite that would bring down quantities of the goldbearing rock. On either side of the drift, water gurgled loudly in ditches dug to drain it to the sump from which the pumps would draw it to the surface.

The head of the drift was glistening dark rock down which water trickled steadily.

The foreman in charge of the drift came forward and touched his hatbrim to Tom Ware.

"She's wet, sir, mighty wet," he said, "and getting worse all the time."

"My engineer says there are some springs in the rock, like we've run into before, nothing to worry about," Ware replied.

"Guess he's right," said the foreman, adding diffidently, "The other mines are having some trouble, too, I been told. More water than they used to get. Not so bad as ours, but more."

"The pumps will take care of it," Ware

answered cheerfully. "Let it squirt."

Walt Slade gazed thoughtfully at the drift head, noting that the trickles which began almost against the roof were larger than those close to the floor of the drift. They made strange whorls and curlycues as they coursed down the face of the rock, as if the watery fingers were tracing a message in some undecipherable cuneiform script.

"Rock isn't quite so rich back here, but still plenty good," observed Ware. "The drifts boring almost due east turn out the best ore."

Slade nodded, still gazing at the glistening face of the drift head.

"Mr. Ware," he said, "might I make a suggestion?"

"Why, sure, son, go right ahead," said old Tom. "What is it?"

"It's something I learned once, in a mine something like this one," Slade replied. "I suggest that you have a drill boring at least three feet ahead of the surface workings."

"Why?" asked Ware.

"To give warning in case there might be a bigger spring in there than your engineer thinks," Slade explained.

Ware stared at him a moment. "I put every dependence in Clifton Billings, the mine engineer," he said, "but just the same that sounds like good sense to me. No use in everybody getting wetter than they are already."

He beckoned the foreman and ordered him to do what Slade suggested.

The foreman, a grizzled old-timer who had been standing close enough to overhear what was said, shot El Halcon a peculiar look and nodded his head.

"Sorta had something of the kind in mind myself," he remarked. "Right away, Mr. Ware."

After watching the operations for a few minutes longer, Ware and Slade returned to the cage. They inspected other galleries and all boring north showed an increase in seepage, while those following a more easterly course were comparatively dry.

"Well," said Ware, "I guess you've seen everything interesting. Suppose we go topside and find something to eat. Crawling around in these coyote holes makes me hungry."

Slade offered no objection to that so they made their way to one of the shaft cages and were whisked up to the tunnel which led to the open air.

"Got a good cook," Ware observed as they left the tunnel mouth. "An old Mexican who sure knows how to throw together a prime helping of chuck. Here's the cook shanty.

"Come a-runnin', Estaban," he shouted. "Got a friend of mine with me I want you to meet."

A wrinkled old fellow with youthfully bright eyes stepped from the kitchen smiling.

"Buenos dias, Don Tomaso, I —" he began, then abruptly ceased speaking, his eyes widening as they rested on Ware's companion. He bent his gray head as to a shrine and his lips moved to murmur a single word, *"Capitan!"*

Instantly, however, he recovered his presence of mind and advanced smiling and bowing.

"It is indeed the pleasure, and the honor, to know the *patron's* guest," he acknowledged and extended his hand, diffidently.

Slade shook hands, his usually cold eyes all kindness. "I, too, am honored to meet one whom Mr. Ware holds in esteem," he said. The old Mexican smiled happily and hurried back to the kitchen.

Keen-eyed old Tom Ware had not missed his cook's sudden confusion at seeing Slade but he made no comment.

As they were sitting down at the table, the door opened and a man entered. He was a thin-faced youngish man; Slade judged him to be about his own age, perhaps a little older, but hardly past thirty. He had a nervous bearing and there were dark circles under his brown eyes; his mouth twitched slightly as he glanced questioningly at Slade.

"Hello, Cliff," Ware greeted him. "Come in and set. Want you to know Walt Slade, a friend of mine. Slade, this is Cliff Billings, my mine engineer."

Billings smiled cordially and shook hands with a good grip. He sat down and spread his napkin over his lap.

"Walt did me quite a favor a while back," Ware confided. "I've a notion he saved me from bustin' my fool neck."

"Then I'm grateful to you also, Mr. Slade," Billings said. "I'd feel bad if something happened to Mr. Ware."

Old Estaban and his helper appeared bearing smoking dishes which they placed on the table. Tom Ware eyed the contents with favor. "Help yourselves, fellers, don't stand on ceremony," he invited heartily. "Young fellers are always hungry. Old ones don't do so bad either," he added, heaping his plate. "Cliff, Walt seems to think there might be a bit more water in that lower level drift head than we've been figuring."

"Nonsense!" scoffed Billings. "I don't

mean to be abrupt, Mr. Slade, but I must disagree with you. I explored these hills thoroughly when I took over here. They are of quartz and granite formation, which is not adaptable to underground water systems. Occasional springs are all we have to cope with."

Slade raised his eyes to the engineer's face. "You must know, sir," he said. "Would it be different if the rocks were other than granite or quartz?"

"Certainly, certainly," said Billings. "Limestone or sandstone formations, for instance, are favorable to underground water."

"I see," Slade said. "Knowing all about a thing is a great advantage."

"Yes, yes," Billings replied in his jerky fashion. "It is my trade, Mr. Slade, just as the cattle business is yours. I doubt if I would enjoy much success trying to lasso a steer."

Slade smiled slightly and deftly changed the subject.

The three men ate a leisurely meal. Ware and Billings discussed mining problems while Slade listened. It did not take him long to conclude that Cliff Billings knew his business and was a competent mining engineer. Which conclusion caused the concentration furrow to deepen between El

Halcon's black brows.

Finally Billings glanced at his watch. "Got to get back on the job," he said. "Lots to do, lots to do. Nice to know you, Mr. Slade. Hope you'll stick around. Hope you'll stick around."

Tom Ware nodded his big head when the door had closed on the engineer.

"Cliff's a nice feller and handles his work fine," he said. "Jumpy sort of a jigger; seems to always be a bit nervous. But he's got big responsibilities and I reckon that makes him that way. Now, son, I believe I said before I'd like to throw something in your way. So I've got an offer to make. Like all cowhands, I reckon you don't feel at home off a horse, so I'm going to hand you a job, if you'll take it, that'll keep you in the saddle most of the time when you're working at it. I own the stage line that runs from Coffin to Clarksburg, the railroad town. A lot of valuable stuff travels by way of the coaches. Among other things, we send our bi-weekly clean-up to the railroad by stage, and it amounts to plenty. So I have guards to ride along just in case; ain't never had any trouble, but you never can tell. How'd you like the chore of captaining the guards? Stage makes three trips a week. The rest of the time you'd have to yourself, and the pay'll be a bit better

110

than you can get for following a cow's tail. No hurry, think on it a day or two if you like. This is Tuesday. Next stage trip is Thursday. If the notion looks good, okay, you can start on Thursday."

Slade smoked in silence for a moment or two. The proposition was attractive. It would give him an excuse for remaining in the section and leave him time to continue his investigation of Pancho Graves' alleged gun-running activities, also to deal with the intriguing mystery of what became of the embezzler, Robert Flint. That is if the report from the Professor of Comparative Anatomy turned out to be what Slade felt sure it would.

"It's a nice offer, sir," he told Ware. "I wouldn't be surprised if I take you up on it, but I would like to have another day or two of just taking it easy."

"Fine!" said Ware. "Suit your own convenience. Well, I guess I'd better get back to the office, work to do."

He accompanied Slade to the stable and made sure that all of Shadow's wants had been adequately taken care of.

"Be seeing you, son," he said as the Ranger rode off. When Slade was some distance down the road, instead of immediately repairing to his office, he returned to the dining room where the old cook was clearing the table.

"Estaban," he said, "I've a notion you know that young feller who was just here. Yes?"

"*Si, Patron,* I have seen him, and of him I have heard much," the cook replied.

"Well, who and what is he?" Ware asked.

"He is a strange man," Estaban returned slowly. "He comes as does the wind, and as the wind he goes. From whence he comes none can say, nor whither he goes. Where people are in trouble or sorrow or fear he appears. And when he departs, the trouble, the sorrow and the fear depart also and are replaced by gladness, peace and content. He has killed men, yes, but none but who deserved death. There are some, and they are evil, who say that he is *El Diablo* from the Pit. Others, and they are many, will tell you that he is as our blessed Lord in the days of old, in that he goes about doing good. *Patron,* they are right."

Tom Ware gazed curiously at the old man, who as he spoke the last words had again bowed his head as to a shrine.

"Estaban, you're right, he's a strange man," Ware said soberly. "And when those eyes of his look at you, you get the feeling that they're looking right inside you, and if there's any dark places you don't want light let into, look out! Yes, a strange man, but there's something about him that gets under your skin in a hurry."

CHAPTER 10

Walt Slade rode back to Coffin slowly, for he was deep in thought. "Shadow," he said as they neared the town, "when that fellow Billings discussed matters with Tom Ware, he gave the impression that he knows his business, but why the devil did he make that fool statement that underground water systems are never found in a quartz or granite terrain? Conditions are less favorable for water eating out a course through granite or quartz formations, but such systems do exist in a quartz or granite terrain, as any engineer worth his salt knows perfectly well. And when he said he had explored these hills and had not run onto limestone or sandstone, he was either blind or was talking through his hat. To the north, limestone and traprock are all that obtain. I can't say for sure how far east those formations run, but I'm much of the opinion that they do so clear to the eastern terminus of the upheaval, the end of the hills to you. I can't understand how Billings could make such a blunder. Oh well, doubtless he's right about the seepage into the mine being caused by some springs in the rock. Just the same, though, I'm glad Ware agreed to drive that drill ahead of the working on the drift face. If there is more than a little water back there, it may save some of those fellows from getting drowned, which is just what would happen if a large volume of water rushed into the drift. Wouldn't need to be very large, either, in that narrow tunnel."

As to whether Shadow thoroughly understood this dissertation on petrology and hydrology is open to debate, but he nodded his head and looked wise. Slade chuckled and rode on to the stable.

During the course of the afternoon, Slade investigated the location of the Square Deal saloon. The building fronted Chaparro Street, its rear on a narrow alley that ran parallel to the main stem. He noted that a back door opened onto the alley, doubtless from a back room. Which fact he stored in his mind for possible future reference.

Slade's interest in the Square Deal was more than casual. It was evidently the hangout of Pancho Graves and his bunch when they happened to be in town, which, Slade gathered, was frequently. So far he felt he had gotten exactly nowhere in his efforts to learn something concerning Graves' alleged gun-running activities. He debated riding east to where Graves' small ranch was located and giving the terrain a once-over, but decided to postpone the trip for a few days. Graves appeared to be hanging around Coffin of late, which Slade considered he would not do if he contemplated running a pack train of contraband goods to the Rio Grande in the near future. He was anxious to keep an eye on Graves and endeavor to anticipate his moves. With this in mind he dropped in at the Square Deal a couple of hours after dark.

He found the saloon crowded but orderly. Every department was doing a good business. The bar was packed, the dance floor echoing to the sprightly click of high heels and the ponderous thudding of boots. Roulette wheels whirred and the gaming tables were occupied. Cole Young, at the far end of the bar, spotted The Hawk's tall form and nodded and smiled. Slade found a space at the bar and bought a drink. Glass in hand, he glanced around the room with interest. He did not see the man he sought, Pancho Graves, but he did see Blaine Gulden sitting in a poker game at a nearby table. The profile of a man sitting next to

Gulden appeared vaguely familiar. The owner of the profile turned in his chair and Slade recognized Cliff Billings, Tom Ware's mining engineer.

Slade was a trifle surprised to see the Last Nugget engineer in the Square Deal, knowing as he did Tom Ware's opinion of the place and its owner. However, he reflected, Billings had a right to go where he pleased during his off hours and perhaps he didn't share Ware's antipathy for Cole Young. And the Square Deal had a reputation for running straight games.

From where he stood, Slade could watch the play at the table. He noted that Billings' face was flushed, his eyes glowing and he appeared more fidgety than usual. He squinted at his cards and his lips moved as if he were muttering to himself.

Very quickly, Slade decided that Cliff Billings had the gambling fever and had it bad. And, as is too often the case in those afflicted by that particular curse, he was losing. The stacks of chips in front of him steadily decreased in height until in a big pot he deposited his last counter, and lost.

His nervous mouth working, he glanced at the wooden-faced dealer who nodded and shoved several tall stacks across the table to Billings, and a slip of paper upon which he wrote a few words. Billings scrawled something on the slip, presumably his signature, and passed it back to the dealer who glanced at it, then slipped it into the table drawer.

Slade gazed thoughtfully at the engineer. The inference of the transaction was plain: Billings had credit at the Square Deal. Slade sipped a drink and ordered another; before he finished it, Billings lost the chips in front of him and signed for more from the dealer. That worthy passed them over without hesitancy and without a questioning glance at Cole Young. He evidently had orders to let Billings have whatever he wanted, or so it appeared.

The press at the bar had thinned somewhat and Slade, being much taller than the average, could see the table and its occupants reflected in the back-bar mirror. He turned his back to the game and continued to watch the play without appearing to do so, turning his attention to Blaine Gulden. He saw that Gulden, who played his own cards in a lackadaisical fashion, was also watching the engineer's play, a look of cynical amusement on his face. Something caused him to glance toward the bar and for an instant his attention remained fixed, directed, Slade knew, at himself.

Slade was startled at the sudden metamorphosis Gulden's countenance underwent. His lips drew back thin against his teeth, his eyes gleamed agate-bright between narrowed lids.

Only for a flickering instant did that expression of malignant hatred shadow Blaine Gulden's features; then it was gone and his handsome face was again impassive as he turned his attention back to the cards.

Walt Slade drew a deep breath. Now he knew where he had seen Blaine Gulden before. His were the passion-distorted features, limned in the blaze of a gun, of the man who had reeled back under the slashing blow of Slade's gun barrel as he tore through the demoralized ranks of the dynamite-packing bunch the night of his arrival at Coffin. So the Graves gang was mixed up in that business, whatever it was!

Well, there was nothing particularly surprising about that, but where the devil were they packing a dozen horse-loads of dynamite through the hills in the dead of night, and for what purpose? Slade didn't have the answers.

As he continued to regard the poker game, Slade stifled a grin. There was a certain element of humor in the situation. If Gulden had recognized him in turn, and it seemed he had, it was not remarkable that he felt a mite unfriendly toward the man who pistol whipped him and split his scalp.

But Slade did not underestimate the glitter-eyed smuggler. Gulden would be out to even up the score did an opportunity offer. Explained now, or so Slade thought, was the attempt to drygulch him back in the hills. Gulden, thoroughly aroused, had doubtless set the little reptile on his trail. One of the fatuous acts even the shrewdest will commit when in the grip of anger. For Gulden must have known, and Graves, too, if Gulden had taken the smuggler leader in his confidence, that in case of a slip-up, such as did occur, that the fellow would be recognized as a member of their bunch.

Of course, however, Graves and Gulden could deny any connection with the attempt, insisting that the man must have been trying to pay off a private grudge. Be that as it might, they would certainly have realized that they were taking the chance of notifying Slade that they were on his trail. Well, all that was water under the bridge and meant only what he already knew, that he must keep a sharp eye on the Graves gang and not let them get him at a disadvantage.

Slade had been casting an occasional

glance at Cole Young standing at the end of the bar and conversing with several men there. He saw Young turn, open the door that led to a back room and close it behind him. A few minutes later a swamper paused at the poker table and said something to Blaine Gulden who nodded.

Gulden played out the hand, stacked his chips and left the table. He headed for the back-room door and disappeared through it. Slade gazed at the closed door, his eyes thoughtful. Looked like a conference of some kind might be going on in the back room. He hesitated, emptied his glass and strolled out. Walking slowly down the street, he made sure that he was not followed, turned the corner and did not pause until he was abreast of the alley than ran in back of the Square Deal. Nobody turned the corner after him and the side street appeared to be deserted. He turned into the alley and made his way cautiously along in the shadow of blank walls on either side. A few more slow steps and he saw a gleam of light which he reasoned must come from one of the saloon windows. Watchful and alert he stole forward until he reached the window. The shade was up a few inches from the bottom. Inching ahead a little more, he was able to peer into the room.

Seated at a table were Cole Young, Blaine Gulden and three men he recognized as members of the Graves bunch. They appeared to be holding earnest conversation, but the window was down and Slade was disappointed in not being able to hear what was said; only a low murmur came to his ears. He wondered if he might he able to hear better with his ear against the nearby door and was edging past the window when a slight sound behind him caused him to whirl around. As a result, the vicious slashing stroke of a gun barrel caught him a glancing blow on the side of the head, which the thick felt of his hat deflected.

Nevertheless the shock was terrific; lights blazed before his eyes and he reeled sideways, caught his balance and managed to grip a descending wrist before another blow could be struck. His other hand shot out and fixed on a throat, drowning a shout to a strangled squawk.

The owner of the gun twisted and writhed, trying to free his wrist, but El Halcon's steely fingers held on and forced the arm up and back as his left hand tightened its grasp on the other's throat. They whirled sideways and by the light from the window, Slade caught a glimpse of a square, distorted face and glowing eyes and recognized Pancho Graves. He put forth every atom of his strength to retain his grip on Graves' throat, knowing that one yell woud bring his henchmen pouring from the room.

Graves lashed out with his free hand and caught Slade a hard blow on the jaw, hurling him back against the wall. Slade ducked his head against the other's chest and a second blow landed on the top of his head and was cushioned somewhat by his hat. He strove to tighten his grip still more and at the same time keep Graves' gunhand up.

He succeeded in doing so, but he couldn't keep Graves from pulling the trigger. The shot boomed out like thunder in the quiet night. Inside the back room sounded the crash of overturned chairs and a thudding of boots. The situation was desperate and Slade took a last desperate chance. He let go of Graves' throat and struck, with all his two hundred pounds of muscle behind the blow. His arm jarred to the elbow as his fist connected. Graves gave a grunt and his big body sagged. Slade jerked on his wrist with all his might and as Graves lunged forward, let go. Even as he bounded up the alley, Graves' body crashed against the wall and floundered to the ground. Slade raced ahead on flying feet.

Behind him the saloon door banged open

and excited voices filled the air. A roaring curse boomed up, doubtless from the throat of Pancho Graves, and a gun banged, again and again.

Slade heard the slugs buzz like angry hornets, one so close that he felt the wind of its lethal breath. A fusillade of reports followed, but El Halcon had whizzed around the corner and was on his way to brightly lighted Chaparro Street at a dead run. At the next corner he slowed down, breathless but exultant. He had escaped from as hot a spot as he recalled ever having been on.

Slade walked on, rubbing his sore jaw where Graves' fist had connected and his equally sore head where his quick turn and the thickness of his hat had saved him from a lethal stroke of that slashing gun barrel. He chuckled as he thought of what must be going on in the back room of the Square Deal at the moment. He doubted if Graves had gotten a good look at him, his face having been in the shadow during the short but fierce struggle, but it was quite probable that the smuggler chief had guessed his identity. Graves and Gulden about now were fit to be tied.

Just the same, Slade was more than a little chagrined over what happened. He knew that he had only himself to blame for his sore head and sore jaw and was ready to admit that his escape from death or serious injury had been largely due to good luck, nothing more. He should have known that somebody might be using the back door to enter the room where Young evidently held conferences and have taken precautions. Absorbed in what was going on beyond that lighted window, he had forgotten all about such a contingency and had come close to paying dearly for his carelessness. Oh well, everybody slipped up at times, but in an affair such as this one, about one slip was all that was permitted; he'd be more careful in the future, or hoped he would.

He reached the swinging doors of the Square Deal and without hesitancy pushed his way through them and strolled to the bar about half way down toward the closed door that led to the back room. He was toying with a drink when the door opened and Blaine Gulden came out, looking anything but in a good temper. Gulden glanced around the room, his gaze fixed on El Halcon's tall form looming well above most of the other bar patrons. His jaw dropped and he halted in his tracks. For a moment he stared, then turned and hastily retraced his steps to the back room. Slade grinned, placed his empty glass on the bar and sauntered out.

CHAPTER 11

In the back room of the Square Deal there was wrath and something resembling consternation. Pancho Graves, a knot on the side of his jaw the size of an egg, his throat swollen and blotched with purple marks, was swearing steadily.

"Blast it, I told you I didn't get a look at his face!" he barked angrily. "I just saw a jigger squattin' down and peepin' in the window, so I took a swipe at him with my gun barrel. He must have heard me or something for he spun around and I didn't get in a good lick. Then he was all over me. When he straightened up, I knew by his height and the size of him he couldn't be anybody else but that infernal El Halcon. I tried to get loose and I tried to yell, but he darn near busted my arm and my neck both. All I could do was pull trigger so you hellions would know something was going on out back. Then all of a sudden he turned me loose and hit me. I thought the roof had fell on me. I cut loose at him as he streaked it up the alley but I was mighty wobbly and couldn't have hit the side of a barn except by plumb luck."

"And the nerve of that sidewinder, to walk right back in and belly up to the bar!" exclaimed Gulden. "I thought I'd tumble over when I saw him."

"He's liable to do anything, as I told you before," growled Graves, caressing his jaw gingerly. "What I want to know is what he was doing out there peeking through the window. You sure that window was down, Young?"

"It was down," Cole Young replied. "He couldn't have heard anything. And I think you're all worrying about him too much. Chances are he was just looking for a chance to even up for the drygulching Pete must have tried to hand him back in the hills."

"And that's nothing to worry about, eh?" snorted Graves. "How do we know which one he was hoping to line sights with through that window? Nothing to worry about!"

"I didn't mean it the way it sounded," Young protested.

"Oh, I know you didn't," retorted Graves. "All you think about is that blasted loco scheme of yours."

"That loco scheme will make you rich," Young replied.

"Or end up getting me six feet of ground three feet down," grunted Graves.

"Say, come to think of it," said one of the men at the table, "this morning I saw that sidewinder riding up to the Last Nugget Mine."

"The devil you did!" ejaculated Young. "What was he doing up there?"

"I wouldn't know," the speaker drawled laconically. "I didn't ask him."

Young shot him an angry glare from his one eye and drummed on the table top with nervous fingers. He turned to the informant.

"Russ, slip out back and see if he's still in the saloon," he directed. "If he isn't, haul Billings out of that poker game and bring him in here."

The man nodded and slid out the back door. Several minutes passed with the group sitting in moody silence. Then the door leading into the saloon opened and Russ reappeared, ushering in Cliff Billings, the Last Nugget mine engineer.

"He ain't nowhere in sight," said Russ. "Here's Billings."

Cole Young wasted no time. "Billings," he said, "this morning did you happen to see a big tall jigger dressed like a cowhand fooling around up at the mine?"

"Why, yes, a fellow answering that description was up there this morning. He was in the cook shanty when I went in for something to eat, having a snack with Tom Ware. They'd just come up out of the mine."

"What!" exclaimed Young.

"That's right," said Billings, "they'd been down at the lower level. Funny, Ware said the fellow, Slade I believe his name is, was saying he believed there might be more water back of that drift head than we thought."

Young jumped in his chair. Pancho Graves swore. Both glared at Billings, who looked frightened.

"But I steered him away from that," Billings hastened to assure them. "I told him he was talking nonsense and explained how there could never be much water in such a formation. I made it convincing and he didn't argue. Anyhow, could a cowhand know anything about such matters?"

"*If* he's just a cowhand," remarked Gulden.

"Blast it, we don't know for sure what he is!" exclaimed Graves. "I'm getting more worried all the time."

"He looked like a cowhand," Billings put in feebly.

"Uh-huh," observed Gulden, his thin lips twisting in a sneer. "And you *look* like an honest engineer."

Billings' nervous mouth twitched and his eyes had a hunted expression.

"Never mind spatting at each other, that'll get us nowhere," said Young. "Billings, how soon do you figure something should happen?"

"Should be very soon, now, from the way things look, most any day, I'd say," Billings replied.

Young nodded. "Keep a close watch on everything, no slips," he said. "And you might try and find out from Ware why that fellow Slade came to see him. Be careful how you go about it, though."

He drew some slips of paper from his pocket as he spoke and riffled them between his fingers.

"Understand you've already dropped another four hundred at the game tonight," he observed with apparent irrelevance. "You're getting in pretty deep."

Billings wet his lips with a nervous tongue and his mouth twitch became more pronounced.

"But don't let it bother you," Young added. "Soon you'll be in a position to take care of everything and not miss it — that is, if everything goes off as expected."

His single gleaming eye fixed on Billings'

face as he spoke and the engineer went livid.

"Everything will come off as planned," he said in a thick voice.

"I hope so," Young said softly, his eye boring into Billings'. The engineer again looked frightened.

CHAPTER 12

After a good night's rest, Slade visited the Last Nugget stamp mill and found Tom Ware in his office.

"Well," said the mine owner, "what's the answer, son?"

"I'll take the job, and thank you very much, sir," Slade replied.

"Good!" exclaimed Ware. "That's fine! Stage leaves here tomorrow morning at nine o'clock. Lays over a day in Clarksburg and then back to Coffin and a lay-over here. Hope you'll like the chore."

"I've a notion I will," Slade replied with a smile.

"Like to give the mill a once-over?" Ware suggested.

Slade was agreeable and they made a tour of the busy establishment, Ware explaining the processes in detail. Slade listened respectfully and mostly in silence. Thoroughly familiar with the workings of a quartz mill, he was more interested in the workers, many of whom were Mexicans. More than once a humble toiler paused in his task to bow his head and smile as the tall form of El Halcon passed. Slade's answering nod and smile were all kindness.

"El Halcon! the friend of the lowly!" would be the murmured exclamation.

The mill manager accompanied them on their tour of the mill. They were standing beside one of the thundering stamp batteries when Ware was called away for a moment.

"How is the output?" Slade asked.

"Excellent," the manager replied. He glanced over his shoulder and saw that his employer was out of earshot. "But it would be better if they'd stop sending us that infernal rock from the north drifts," he added peevishly. "The gold content doesn't pay the cost of working it. I don't see why Ware keeps driving those galleries north. I've told him the rock is no good, but he says Billings insists that indications show they're almost sure to strike big pockets of valuable ore at any time. In my opinion Billings is making a mistake."

"Anybody can make mistakes," Slade commented.

"No doubt about that," grunted the manager, "and I figure this time Billings is making a mighty costly one. Funny darn rock, too. Not true quartz. Almost as if limestone was mixed in it."

"It very likely is," Slade said. The manager shot him a questioning glance, but Slade did not elaborate and before the manager could pursue the subject, Tom Ware rejoined them and the conversation ceased.

Slade walked back to his room puzzling over Cliff Billings' peculiar behavior. The engineer must know that the rock through which he was driving the north galleries was of very meager gold content, really not worth working; but of course his theory of rich pockets of ore being possible at any time was substantiated by mining experience; although the type of rock he was encountering made such a strike highly unlikely.

Slade gathered that the mill manager had protested to him, as perhaps his experienced foreman had also done. And like many weak men, Billings might have a stubborn streak and a fatuous idea that opposition, sometimes to the extreme of plain contrariness, was a sign of strength. That might explain it. Slade believed there was more water somewhere in the rock to the north than Billings did, but Billings' contention that it came from big springs had plenty of examples to back his opinion. Slade felt confident that if they broke through suddenly and released the flow of the springs, the miners were in for a good wetting, but with his suggestion of drilling three feet ahead of the drift face being followed, there should be ample warning of any undue accumulation in some hollow or natural tunnel in the rock.

What Slade pondered more seriously was Billings' apparent association with Cole Young and presumably with Blaine Gulden, although Gulden might have been sitting in the poker game by chance. Slade felt that no good would come of it for the engineer. But that was Billings' business and if he was going to gamble it had might as well be in a place bearing a reputation for straight games. A player afflicted by the fever as Billings evidently was had enough to contend with without bucking a crooked deal.

At nine o'clock the following morning the Clarksburg stage pulled out of Coffin. The stage was a great swaying, rocking cradle on wheels drawn by six mettlesome horses. It was lined with boiler iron, the narrow windows were barred and there were heavy locks on the doors. An armed guard sat beside the driver and two more were ensconced inside the armored coach.

Slade rode beside the off leader, where he could scan the road ahead. He was alert but did not really expect trouble. The terrain was not favorable for outlaw operations, the road curving around the base of the hills all the way to Clarksburg but never drawing very close to them and with the open desert to the south replaced farther east by even more open rangeland. And the armored and heavily-guarded coach would be a tough nut to crack. It was possible that a reckless bunch might make a try for the vehicle when it was known to be packing a valuable gold shipment from the mines, but on routine trips Slade believed there was little cause for apprehension.

Nevertheless, his habitual caution was not relaxed. He studied every thicket and outcropping of chimney rocks within rifle range and his gaze constantly roved over the dark hills to the north. In this land the unexpected was what all too frequently happened; best not to take chances.

However, the trip was made without incident and the stage pulled up at the Clarksburg station in the afternoon. Clarksburg proved to be a typical Texas cattle town with long lines of loading pens flanking the railroad sidings and dominated by the old fort which sat on a rise. There were blue clad cavalrymen on the streets, rubbing shoulders with cowboys from the spreads or drinking with them in the saloons. Slade surveyed the fort with interest and put it in the back of his mind for possible future reference.

Slade enjoyed the lay-over at Clarksburg. After Coffin's turbulence the comparative calm of the cow town was relaxing. He sauntered about the busy streets, had a drink now and then and played a few hands of poker with some rowdy but good-natured punchers and equally spirited soldiers of about the same age. The dance-floor girls were congenial and better looking than most. Clarksburg wore a cheerful air modified by the dignity of long existence. The cow town had gotten over its "growing pains" many years before. The whistles of the trains rumbling past enhanced Clarksburg's aura of civilization, although Slade decided it could paw sod a bit should the occasion arise.

The trip back to Coffin was equally without untoward happenings. Slade's first chore upon arriving at the mining town was to visit the post office. As he had expected, he found there a letter from the Professor of Comparative Anatomy at Baylor University. He repaired to his room over the stalls before reading it.

Skull in question is of Mongolian type. *Not* Caucasian. American Indian. Presumably of Western Tribe.

"Just as I thought," he remarked aloud. "Robert Flint was not killed by Apaches. Those bones belonged to an Apache *he* killed."

Rolling and lighting a cigarette, he reconstructed what must have happened. The Apaches drygulched Flint, all right, but he somehow managed to fight them off, killing one and possibly wounding others. Evidently, however, he was badly hurt himself; the evidence of a number of campfires indicated that he had spent quite a few days at the spot, doubtless recovering from his wounds and building enough strength to travel, possibly remaining until his food supply was exhausted. Being able to build the fires indicated that his wounds were not of a fatal nature and very likely by the time he was ready to move he was well on the road to recovery. Where did he go? That was a question, but Slade was of the opinion he had continued north by east. If he was at all familiar with the section, he would have known that Clarksburg and the railroad lay in that direction. Very unlikely that he would have turned back south on the chance of meeting up with his former companion, Tom Ware. And behind him lay the desert, a hazardous crossing for even a man in good health and with plenty of supplies. His burro had been killed and he was entirely on his own. Civilization would certainly have been his objective. What had become of him after that? Slade didn't have the answer. The only man he had contacted in Coffin who at all fitted the description given by Tom Ware and Edward Duncan was Blaine Gulden, and Slade rather doubted that Gulden and Flint were the same, although of course it was not impossible. He was still of the opinion that Tom Ware would pass a clean-shaven Flint on the street and fail to recognize him. Well, after all, he, Slade, was in Coffin primarily to try and tie up Pancho Graves with arms smuggling across the Rio Grande, and Graves couldn't smuggle arms and hang around the mining town at the same time. Looked like in everything he was getting nowhere fast.

"All I've been able to tie onto so far is a sore jaw and a sore head," he growled disgustedly. "But where the devil was that pack train load of dynamite going and for what? I still figure that's worth trying to find out. And all of a sudden I got a notion that may give me a line on Flint."

Slade laid over a day in Coffin and then accompanied the stage on its next trip to Clarksburg. This time he did not loaf aimlessly about the town but at once proceeded to put his "notion" into effect; he headed for the fort and requested an interview with the post commander, which was readily granted.

The major in command proved to be a pleasant looking elderly man who invited him to sit down.

"Well, what can I do for you, young fellow?" he asked. "Somebody been stealing your cows?"

"Nope, haven't any to be stolen," Slade smiled reply. He drew something from a cunningly concealed secret pocket in his broad leather belt as he spoke and laid it on the commander's desk. The major stared at the famous silver star set on a silver circle, the feared and honored badge of the Texas Rangers.

"So that's it!" he exclaimed. "What's up?"

"I don't know for sure," Slade admitted, "but if you will answer a few questions it may help me to find out."

"Fire away," replied the officer. "Always glad to do anything I can to help the Rangers."

After requesting secrecy, which the major readily promised, Slade outlined what he knew of Robert Flint and the description given him. At first the results were not at all sanguine. The major kept shaking his head.

"Every now and then we have an injured man come to the post seeking help," he explained, "but I do not recall one answering your description of the man Flint. But, say! I believe you said that was about five years back, right? I've only been here a little over four. Wait a minute."

He summoned an orderly. "Find Sergeant O'Keefe and send him here," he directed. Shortly a weatherbeaten old regular who looked as if he had served under General Washington and in every war since the Revolution put in an appearance. He listened intently to Slade's description.

"Sure, Major," he said at length, "I've a notion that might have been the feller who wrung the *paisano* bird's neck."

"*Paisano* bird?" repeated the major.

"Yes, sir — a chaparral cock or road runner as they call 'em hereabouts. That was about five years back, all right, a week or ten days after we had the brush with Laughing Bear over in the hills and he got away from us. A feller who looked sort of like the one you're talking about came staggering up to the post all shot to pieces — left arm busted, one eye gone and part of his nose, and the side of his face smashed in. Must have come mighty near to hearing the banshee wail. Said the Injuns got him, very likely Laughing Bear and his bunch. The sawbones — beg your pardon, Major — the post surgeon patched him up and we nursed him back into shape. He got his strength back, but I've a feeling the slug that knocked his eye out did something to his brains, too; always had a wild look in his one eye."

"Sergeant," Slade interrupted, "you're sure of the exact nature of the wounds?"

"I'm sure," replied O'Keefe. "I helped the saw— the post surgeon patch him up. And getting on to the road runner — that's one reason why I figured the feller must have gotten bats in his garret. One of the boys had made a pet of one of those long-legged scooters. The feller I'm talking about saw it one day and started bawlin' cuss words and made a dive for it. Before anybody could stop him, he'd wrung the poor critter's neck. Kept saying that one of the infernal things was to blame for all his trouble. There was a row, of course, and he left the post that night, and that's the last anybody ever seen or heard of him so far as I know. Feller must have had plenty of money in a belt he wore under his shirt. Before he left, he flung two twenty-dollar yellow boys on a bunk and told the feller who owned the road runner to go buy another of the blasted hoodoos to take the place of the one he killed. That's all I know, sir."

"Thank you, Sergeant, very much," Slade said. "You've been a great help."

O'Keefe saluted and left the room. Slade turned to the major.

"Yes, a great help," he repeated.

The officer regarded him curiously. "And you think what O'Keefe told you may enable you to locate Flint?" he asked.

"Yes, I think I can locate him," Slade replied. "But I'm hanged if I know what to do with him."

Chapter 13

Slade left the commander's office thoroughly disgusted with himself. The same old story — hunt all over Hades for something and all the while it's right under your nose! For Slade did not for a moment doubt that Cole Young and Robert Flint were one and the same. Flint minus an eye, his hair prematurely grayed, and with a frightfully scarred face, and a mind perhaps somewhat unbalanced by his sufferings. No wonder Tom Ware had failed to recognize him.

Well, anyhow, the Flint angle was taken care of and the establishment of the fund to aid needy dependents of Rangers who lost their lives in the duty assured. Edward Duncan could contact his larcenous former associate and, circumstances being what they were, would doubtless have no trouble getting his signature to certain papers necessary to the business transactions he had in mind. Finding Flint in such comfortable circumstances, he might insist on restitution of the money Flint purloined, but he had positively declared that he had no intention of prosecuting Flint; so as a Ranger, Slade had no further interest in Cole Young as Robert Flint.

But he did have a very definite interest in Cole Young as Cole Young. The Square Deal owner's background being what it had proved to be, his association with Pancho Graves and his bunch acquired significance. He might be assisting Graves in his smuggling operations, making that pest doubly dangerous, providing as he did, what Slade had already concluded Graves lacked, a keen brain capable of planning and carrying out intricate operations which were beyond the smuggler's limited intelligence. With Young pulling the strings and Graves and Blaine Gulden as his field men, there was no telling what the scampish trio might be able to do. The gun running which the Rangers were anxious to stop abruptly assumed formidable proportions.

But Slade had an uneasy premonition that Young might be up to something more outstanding. He believed Young would look on smuggling as small potatoes, its limited remuneration unworthy of his talents. But what the devil could he have in mind? Slade didn't know the answer but he was convinced that in some way the large quantity of dynamite being transported through the hills by Graves' gang would play a part.

The evening the stage arrived in Coffin on the return trip to the mining town, disaster struck. Deep in the gloomy lowest drift the hard-rock men were still driving north. The blasts that would be fired when the day shift went off duty had been set, the fuses ready to light, when suddenly the drill that steadily bored three feet ahead of operations shot from the hole with prodigious force. There followed a jet of water hard as steel that knocked down and badly bruised several men. A plug previously prepared was with great difficulty driven into the hole, stopping the flow of water.

But the old foreman in charge of the hard-rock gang held up his hand.

"Don't light those fuses," he ordered. "I'm going to see Billings; he's down here somewhere."

The foreman found Billings without difficulty and laid the case before him.

"There's a lot of water back there, sir," he concluded. "The way that drill shot out proves it. May be more than we think."

Billings' nervous mouth twitched. "Didn't I order you to keep on driving till I told you to stop?" he demanded irritably. "If there's water back there we've got to drain it off eventually. The pumps will take care of it. Go ahead and fire your blasts. I'll tell you when to stop driving."

The foreman touched his hat in silence and went back to his men.

"Just the same I don't like it," he grumbled. "Loose those fuses and replace them with longer ones. When they're fired, everybody head for the cage. I want everybody away from here before that powder cuts loose."

The miners obeyed and were well down

the tunnel before the dull booming of the exploding dynamite sounded. It was followed by a mighty crashing and thudding.

"They brought down the whole drift face," muttered the foreman.

They had, but that wasn't all. Echoing the crashes came an ominous roaring that swelled and swelled, shaking the tunnel walls, smiting the ear as the diapason of hammered steel.

"Scoot!" shouted the foreman. "We've tapped the whole blasted Rio Grande!"

Down the tunnel the miners fled at a dead run. Before they had covered a hundred yards, water was sloshing about their ankles. It rose to their knees, and when they reached the shaft and the lifting cage it was thigh deep. Breathless and panting they piled onto the platform which was covered with water. The foreman frantically jangled the signal wire.

"If something fouls, we're done for!" he gasped and continued to tug at the wire.

The cables hummed, the cage creaked and groaned under the accumulated weight of the water. It rose a little, jerked to a stop. The roar of the flood rushing down the tunnel was now a mighty thunder. Glancing through the darkness dimly illumined by the cap lights, the foreman saw a pale vision of horror rushing toward them. He gave a howl of despair.

The cage jerked again, sagged drunkenly, almost stopped, then slowly it began to rise as the water poured off. Two feet, three, it slowed still more, seemed to hang suspended, then shot upward. Below sounded a liquid crashing as the black water raved and bellowed at the escape of its victims.

"Get everybody out!" yelled the foreman the instant his feet touched the floor of the tunnel leading to the open air. "Get 'em out! You haven't any time to waste."

Cliff Billings came rushing forward. "There's no danger," he chattered. "The flow will soon stop!"

"Soon stop, the devil!" bawled the foreman. "It'll be running out this tunnel before it stops. Blast you! Give the orders to get the men out or I'll break you in two!"

He started for the engineer, his gnarled hands opening and shutting. Billings turned white and without more ado began shouting the necessary orders. For a moment there was near panic, then the old foreman took over and quieted the turmoil. Telegraph signals rang deep in the mine. The cages began rising to the surface loaded with men; but it was slow work, and ever the awesome rumble in the depths of the mine loudened, interspersed with distant crashings.

"The north end of the mine is caving in," said the miners arriving to the surface. "And weak spots in the gallery roofs are liable to give way."

The mine siren began to shriek. Other mine whistles joined in till the air quivered with their eerie wailing. Engineers and officers of the other mines, realizing something was wrong, started flocking to the Last Nugget, as did people from the town.

Walt Slade arrived in the forefront. Sitting his tall horse he listened to the excited gabbling. He spotted Cliff Billings, pale and shaken, explaining to a group of engineers what had happened.

"Here comes Mr. Ware," somebody shouted. "He'll know what to do."

Mr. Ware didn't know what to do, nor did anybody else. Wild conjectures flew about.

"It'll soon run off, it'll soon run off," Cliff Billings kept repeating. Nobody heard or heeded him.

Tom Ware saw Slade lounging in his saddle at the outskirts of the crowd and walked over to join him.

"Son," he said, his voice shaking a little, "if it hadn't been for you, a dozen men in that low-level north drift would have been drowned. That drilling ahead you suggested saved them."

Slade nodded but did not otherwise comment.

"I don't know what the devil to do," Ware said. "The water keeps rising and rising with no signs of stopping. The boys from the other pits don't know what to do, either."

"I'd suggest," Slade said dryly, "that they hustle back to their own workings, pull all the men from the lower levels except for a skeleton force of masons and begin building retaining walls in the north drifts against the possibility that they'll catch it, too."

"I believe you're right," said Ware. "Wait here for me." He hurried away and began talking with the group of officials and engineers. Tom Ware's words carried weight and the group quickly dispersed as each hurried back to his own station to put Slade's suggestion into effect. Ware returned to El Halcon.

"It may not be necessary for them to take the precaution, but I figure it's best not to risk it," Slade said. "This is a strange occurrence, sir. Only once in mining annals has anything resembling it occurred, to the best of my knowledge. The single paralleling incident, and the parallel is uncanny in similarity, was at the Tombstone silver mines in Arizona. There all the mines are affected.

148

They were thoroughly drowned and remain so to this day. All efforts to draw off the water failed. Here, only the Last Nugget appears to suffer, although of course we can't tell for sure at the moment. It's my opinion, however, that the other mines will not be affected."

"I hope you're right," said Ware, "but what about the Last Nugget?"

"Only time will tell," Slade replied, adding grimly, "but things don't look good right now." He added a word of comfort.

"But if the water stops rising, you'll just have to pump it out."

"But if it continues to rise?" asked Ware.

"Depends on the continuing volume of the rise," Slade answered. "Let's wait and see."

He dismounted, and he and Ware moved to the tunnel mouth.

Suddenly, from the tunnel sounded a louder shouting. A wild-eyed miner burst into view.

"The third drift," he panted to Tom Ware. "Roof fell in — seven men trapped back there!"

Pandemonium ensued, men shouting and screaming and cursing.

"My God! We've got to get them out!" roared Tom Ware.

"It would be suicide to go down there now," chattered Cliff Billings, his face working grotesquely. "I tell you it would be suicide!"

Walt Slade's voice rang out with an authority that stilled the tumult.

"All right," he called, "I want volunteers — a dozen men will do. We'll get them out."

Men began pushing forward. "I'm with you for one," said Tom Ware.

"No," Slade replied. "I want young men — huskies. Mr. Ware, you get together the tools we'll need — picks, bars, shovels. No, no powder. We can't risk a blast — it might bring more roof down. But," he added as an afterthought, "get a length of the strongest rope or wire cable you have, forty or fifty feet, and a couple of stout poles ten feet or so long."

The old foreman of the lowest drift was plucking at Slade's sleeve. "Let me go with you, sir," he pleaded. "I know the mine, better'n anybody here."

"Okay," Slade said, "we'll need somebody with brains and experience. What's your name?"

"Dennis, sir," the other replied.

"Okay, Dennis," Slade repeated. "Check the men I pick out and see if they're all right for the chore; can't let everybody go."

From the swarm of volunteers, Slade chose his men with care, old Dennis nodding approval of each man picked. Five minutes later they swarmed into the tunnel, loaded with the needed tools and equipment. All were able to pack in a single cage which was slowly lowered into the resounding, vibrating mine.

The cage creaked to a stop at the third drift. In the sudden stillness could be heard the sinister gurglings and rustlings of the water that still rose in the lower levels.

"We won't have any time to waste, she's rising fast," Slade said as they hurried along the gallery by the glimmer of the cap lights.

"I don't think the fall will be over broad," said old Dennis. "I know that spot in the roof. Fact is, I spoke to Mr. Billings about it once, but he thought it was okay and didn't put in extra shoring."

"There it is!" somebody shouted as the lights shone on a mass of splintered stone that blocked the gallery from floor to roof.

"Listen!" Slade exclaimed. As the miners hushed their babble, a barely perceptible clicking reached their ears.

"They're trying to dig out," said Dennis. "They'd never make it alone."

Without an instant's delay the miners tore into the mass of fallen rubble. Picks thudded, shovels scraped, brawny arms strained on the crowbars.

But very quickly they ran into difficulties that seemed insurmountable; huge chunks of the fallen rock defied the bars and picks.

"I figured as much, and prepared against it," Slade said. "All right, pass the rope around that big block. Okay, now tie the other end to one of the supporting timbers back here, leave some slack. Bring those poles, Dennis. Twist the slack around one pole half way up, and stand the pole straight on the floor. Now make a loop in the slack and thrust the other pole through it. Right! Now three men on the end of this transverse pole and walk around the upright, winding up the slack."

"By gosh! A Spanish windlass!" exclaimed old Dennis. "Remember seeing one used once, on a grading job."

"Yes, and two men can move a house with that thing, if the transverse pole which is the lever is long enough," Slade said. "See, that hunk of rock is coming out of the mess."

Crunching and grinding, the huge fragment of stone slithered up the gallery floor. The pick and shovel and bar men swarmed forward and rock flew back in a shower until they encountered a second obstacle. Once again, the windlass was brought into play and the big stone yanked in the clear.

"We're doing it, we're doing it!" panted old Dennis as he plied his pick the faster.

"But it's going to be touch and go," Slade said quietly. He gestured to something that moved gleamingly down the tunnel. It was a film of water.

"Rising up the shaft and reaching the gallery," Slade added. "Sift sand, boys, no time to lose."

Faster and faster flew the picks. Harder and harder, muscular arms strained on the bars. Several times more the windlass was brought into play to move fragments too heavy for the bar men to handle. Now the clicking on the far side of the barrier was much louder and answering shouts to the cries of encouragement from the rescuers were clearly heard.

But the water was rising at an alarming rate. It sloshed about the ankles of the perspiring toilers, rose to their knees and crept up and up. Never for an instant, however, did the frantic efforts slacken.

Walt Slade was everywhere at once, figuratively speaking, doing the work of two men, lending his great strength to start stones moving that defied the bars. His shirt was drenched with sweat, his face haggard with strain. It was a fight for life, for a little more water and the rescuers would be as fatally trapped as those behind the fallen roof.

Hurling a large fragment aside, Slade suddenly saw a gleam of light filtering through the cracks between the stones.

"We're through, boys, we're through, that's their cap lights!" he shouted. "Quick, widen the opening."

Picks thudded, shovels scraped, fragment after fragment was hurled aside until there was an opening through which a man wriggled. Another followed him, and another and another, until all seven of the trapped miners were accounted for.

"To the cage!" Slade shouted. "We haven't a minute to spare."

Up the tunnel sloshed the miners, through water now thigh deep. They reached the cage, gasping and panting. The floor of the platform was covered with water and jets geysered up on all sides as the imprisoned flood poured into the upper gallery.

Fortunately the pressure from beneath had raised the cage somewhat; the cables hung loose. Onto the platform scrambled the men, until it was crowded to capacity. And Slade and the old foreman still stood in the rising water on the tunnel floor.

Wordless Slade reached out and tugged

the signal cord. The cage groaned, swayed, started to rise with laboring jerks. The water poured off and it shot upward. Slade turned to old Dennis.

"Maybe," was all he said. Dennis nodded his understanding.

For what seemed an eternity the abandoned pair stood in the rising water, their hearts numbing with despair. The upward surging water had developed a current that all but swept them from their feet. They strained their eyes upward through the dark shaft, and saw nothing, and heard nothing.

"Looks like it's our finish, sir," said Dennis, his voice calm. "Don't matter for an old coot like me, my time wasn't far off anyhow, but it's a shame a young feller like you has to cash in his chips this way."

"We're not dead yet, and till we are we don't worry about it," said Slade. "Listen, don't I hear something?"

He did, the hum and rattle of the cables. Down came the cage, smacking into the water and hanging suspended, swaying and creaking. Slade gripped old Dennis about the waist and hoisted him to the platform. With his last ounce of strength he scrambled up beside the foreman and jerked the signal cord.

Again there was the moment of terrible

suspense as the cables hummed and groaned. Then the cage shot upward. Scant moments later they stepped onto the floor of the tunnel to the accompaniment of deafening cheers from the crowd that choked the bore. Men slapped Slade on the back, whooping and praising, until he began to fear he had escaped death by drowning only to be beaten to death by well meaning admirers.

Tom Ware said nothing; he stepped forward and solemnly shook hands.

"And now what?" he asked some minutes later as they walked to the tunnel entrance. "The infernal water's still rising."

"As I said before, wait and see," Slade replied.

They "waited" and they "saw." The next morning water was flowing from the entrance tunnel. By afternoon it was a raging torrent that choked the bore from floor to roof, scoured out a bed for itself and flowed past Coffin to lose itself in the thirsty sands of the desert, providing the mining town with a brand new river all its own.

Slade was constantly in attendance on Tom Ware, who seemed to lean on him for support and comfort in his hour of trial.

"Billings wants to telegraph for more pumping machinery," the owner confided to Slade.

"Forget it!" El Halcon snapped. "If you set up a pump on every square yard of ground available you couldn't lower the level of that flow, and Billings should know it."

"But what am I going to do?" Ware asked helplessly.

"I'll repeat what I said before — wait," Slade replied.

So they waited. Ware held consultation with the engineers of the other mines. Their verdict was unamimous and gloomy.

"Looks like you tapped an underground river, just as they did over at Tombstone," they said. "Looks like the Last Nugget is a goner."

"And I'm afraid they're right," Ware confided to Slade. "Looks like the things I'd planned for this town have gone down the flume. Oh, I'm not busted — yet. I've got a little money stashed away, not much, for I plowed back most of the profits into the mine, for new machinery, better working conditions and such things. I've still got the stage line, which pays, but the hopes I had for Coffin are done for. Cole Young will take over — now he'll win the councilmanic election for sure — and put his own men in charge of things. He'll turn what I'd in-

157

tended to be a nice community into a heller."

"Perhaps, and then again perhaps not," Slade answered. "Somehow I've a notion that Young is going to make some kind of a move before long. And," he added to himself, "one that may tip his hand. Something mighty, mighty funny about all this. Looks to me like Billings knew just what was coming and made no move to prevent it, and in my opinion Young has got his claw firmly in Billings and Billings jumps when Young pulls the string."

Just where Cole Young fitted into the picture, Slade hadn't the least idea, but he had a hunch that Young was in the picture, very importantly so, and he had learned from experience to respect his hunches.

Meanwhile the engineers of the other mines were working frantically to shore up their north drifts and building retaining walls against what might be imminent danger.

Slade asked a few questions, among them, "Any increase in the flow of water?"

"No," was the answer. "Still just seepage. But we believe you were right in your suggestion, and we're taking no chances."

One or two of the engineers asked some questions of their own.

"You appear to be familiar with such operations, Slade, have you worked in mines? Or on construction projects of some kind?"

"I've been around mines some, and you learn a good deal from experience," Slade replied.

The engineers did not ask him to elaborate; in fact, they asked no more questions, evidently feeling that if they did so, they would not be answered. In which surmise they were correct.

A few days later, Slade's hunch was justified; Cole Young did make a move. He requested an interview with Tom Ware, which was granted. Slade was not present at the conference although Ware had requested him to be.

"I'd rather hear from you what he has on his mind," he explained. "I prefer not to have him notice me any more than he already has."

Young wasted no time when he and Ware met in the mill office.

"I know you and I don't see things eye to eye," he said, "but I figure there's one thing on which we agree; we both want to see this town keep humming. The Last Nugget, as we both know, was far and away the biggest producer and the town is going to miss it, miss it badly. If for no other reason, we want to keep the Last Nugget producing or, rather, to resume producing. I have an idea how to drain off that water and start the mine operating. I have some money corraled and I'm willing to gamble it on what I believe. If I'm wrong, I'm busted. Yes, I'm willing to gamble my money, but I want to be in a position to cash in on the winnings, if there are any. So I'm offering to buy the Last Nugget."

"And what do you offer?" Ware asked.

Ware concealed his anger with difficulty when Young named the price he would pay. It was ridiculously low.

"Tell you tomorrow," Ware said. "I want a night to think it over."

"Okay," said Young, a malicious gleam in his single eye. "Offer holds good till tomorrow."

Old Tom was still wrathful when he contacted Walt Slade a little later. After a tirade against Cole Young, he told Slade what Young had offered. Slade sat silent a moment, then he said, "Sell, and let's see what Young has in mind. I'm of the opinion that he may tip his hand. As I see it, you have nothing to lose and everything to gain."

Ware hesitated and Slade decided it was time to play his trump card.

"Mr. Ware," he said, "I am going to tell you a couple of things, but first I want your pledge of secrecy; I don't want to have generally known what I am going to tell you, not yet."

"It's a deal," nodded the mine owner. "Anything you say will be between you and me."

Slade nodded. "First," he said, "I am a graduate engineer and know what I'm talking about. Secondly —"

He laid the star of the Rangers on the desk between them.

Tom Ware gazed at the symbol of law and order and justice for all. "So that's what you are," he muttered. "Ought to have known it."

"Yes, I'm with Captain McNelty's company," Slade said. "I was sent here from Post headquarters at Patricio on another matter, but I think this mining business merits some Ranger attention."

"Okay," said Ware, "I figure I can't go wrong on a Ranger. I'll do whatever you advise."

"Then sell to Young tomorrow and let him go ahead with whatever he has in mind, and leave the rest to me."

"It's a deal," Ware repeated. "And I've a notion that sidewinder is going to get his come-uppance at last."

Slade hoped Ware was right, but he figured he had his work cut out for him. Unless all signs failed, Cole Young was a formidable opponent for even El Halcon.

CHAPTER 14

The papers were signed the following day and Cole Young became the owner of the Last Nugget mine. Slade wondered what Tom Ware would have said had he known that the man to whom he deeded his property was also the man who had accompanied him across the desert in search of wealth in the grim Tinto Hills.

Cole Young immediately got busy, in an unexpected place and an unexpected manner.

Not far east of Coffin a narrow box canyon bored north into the hills for a considerable distance. Young began driving a tunnel into the box wall of the canyon. There was plenty of supplies and equipment available, and the miners who had lost their jobs when the Last Nugget closed down were eager for work, so that there was an abundance of labor. The work proceeded apace.

The engineers of the other mines were loud in their snorts of derision.

"Sure he can tap the Last Nugget lower galleries, and it won't take him long, either," they admitted, "but a lot of good it will do him. He can't possibly drain off the water as fast as it is flowing into the mine. No matter how wide he drives his tunnel, he can't widen the mine galleries, and the outflow will be limited to the volume of water a single gallery can accommodate. He's loco as a coot and shy of brains as a terrapin is of feathers!"

To which scoffing Young's only answer was, "Wait and see!"

Walt Slade said nothing. He had gathered from Edward Duncan that the absconding Robert Flint was an engineer of no mean ability and he felt confident that Young had an ace up his sleeve. It was up to him to trump that ace when it was played, but how the devil to do so with a hand that so far held no cards! That was the problem that confronted the Ranger.

It was a week after Young began operations that Walt Slade rode into the hills. He left Coffin in the dark and quiet hour that preceded the dawn. Where the west fork of the draw began he paused to make sure he had not been followed and then continued up the west fork. A few hours later he reached the spot where Robert Flint's battle with the Apaches had been fought, and where he, Slade, came close to taking the Big Jump via a drygulcher's bullet. Here he did not pause but rode on steadily.

As the draw began to curve to the east it steadily grew rougher. Its depth increased greatly and the earth and stone sides were replaced by tall cliffs slanting slightly back, absolutely destitute of plants, gray, drab, million-faceted. The steep surfaces had been broken and weathered away by frost and recurrent thaws until they were cracked into millions of pieces, each one of which had both smooth and sharp surfaces. Dull gray in color, and so seamed and cracked and fissured, the dizzy slopes had the appearance of a net of rock, numberless stones of myriad shapes pieced together by some colossal hand, and now split and ready to fall. The rugged, bold, uneven walls shone in the sunlight like a vast splintered mirror, hanging there as if by magic, every one of the heaps of stone leaning ready to roll.

The cliffs towered dark and terrible and forbidding even in the broad light of day. And yet there was a frightful beauty in the unstable mass as the sun gleamed on the uncounted facets, a stark, elemental beauty such as is found only in the raw, sinister manifestations of Nature in an inscrutable mood.

What held that seamed and lined and sundered mass of rock together, Slade wondered. For what was it waiting? He shuddered a little despite the blistering heat of the gulch as a weathered fragment loosened from the crest of a cliff to crack ringingly on the lower slope and bound and hurtle downward with diminishing claps till it ceased with a little hollow report on the floor of the gulch. A warning voice, ominously promising what would happen should the whole unstable mass take a notion to avalanche.

An arid and dangerous waste with nothing to tempt the prospector or casual explorer, or so it would seem. What business would anybody have in such an inferno of heat and continuous threat! Seemed ridiculous to think anybody of sane mind would enter here.

But Slade discovered indubitable evidence that horses had passed this way. Most of the signs were old, but others denoted the quite recent passage of one or two animals.

Slade's interest quickened. What legitimate business *could* anybody have up this dreary and festering wound in the earth's surface? Slade didn't know, but he intended to find out.

For more than a mile the forbidding terrain obtained, then gradually the cliffs lowered and again earth and shale which sprouted stunted brush and flowering weeds resumed sway. Slade rode on, watchful and alert. The horses that had recently passed this way presumed riders, and the nature of said riders was dubious. Slade felt it would be to his interest to spot them before they spotted him. He rode slowly and gave every bristle of bush and clump of boulders his careful attention.

It was past noon when he arrived at the rim of a deep and fairly wide canyon where the wash petered out. Slade pulled up and gazed into the depths of the gorge.

"Shadow," he said, "I never saw anything like that before, and I believe we've struck pay dirt."

The floor of the canyon was a lake. Nothing remarkable about that, for a mile or so to the north was the silvery gleam of a fair-sized stream which fed the lake. But what was remarkable was the fact that here and there appeared the tops of large trees rising above the surface of the water. And the shriveled and rotted condition of the leaves showed that they, too, had been submerged no great time before.

The water was deep, fully fifty feet, Slade estimated, and as the tree tops showed, it had once been much deeper. Which meant, of course, that a large portion of the water which had once filled the canyon nearly to its rim had been drained off.

The canyon ran south with a westerly veering until it merged with the haze of the distances; but something over a mile below where Slade sat his horse it narrowed greatly and the Ranger felt sure the narrowing continued until it finally butted against the higher hill wall not far to the north and east of Coffin and pretty well in line with the mines located on the east fork of the draw.

Rolling a cigarette, Slade lounged comfortably in the saddle and pondered what he had discovered. He believed now he had solved the mystery of the flooded mine and the explanation of Cole Young's extraordinary behavior in driving the tunnel the mine engineers declared could never drain the Last Nugget mine.

But he had to make sure, and to learn where the stream which formed the surprising lake had formerly turned away from the canyon to probably flow east. He spoke to Shadow and headed south by west along the canyon rim.

But the going was hard and progress slow. Mile after mile he covered, while the sun slanted down the western sky and the shades of evening drew near. Night was not far off when he at last reached a point where he could plainly make out the beetling escarpment of the hill wall north of the mines. Above the hill crests, fouling the gold and scarlet of the sunset sky, was the smoke of the mills of Coffin. And nowhere had he found a point where the stream had left the canyon before it had been dammed to form the artificial lake.

A little later, with the shadows curdling in the gorge's depths, he saw that the box end of the now quite narrow canyon was split by the dark mouth of a large cave into which the stream flowed.

"Yes, this is it," he told Shadow, "the back door to the north galleries of the Last Nugget mine. But, horse, I slipped a little and I'll have to pay for it tomorrow with another long ride. I should have ridden north first. Evidently up there beyond the wide section of the canyon the stream was diverted from its original course and turned into the canyon. Until I've made sure of that I have no case. Well, guess you can't do everything right, but things do seem to be turning our way. So we'll just take it easy tonight and continue our investigation tomorrow."

Searching out a thicket around which grass grew, he got the rig off the black horse and turned him loose to graze. A nearby spring provided water and he soon had food cooking and coffee bubbling over a small fire. After eating he stretched out on his blanket, rolled a smoke and pondered the novel and intricate scheme the former engineer who had been Robert Flint and was now Cole Young had evolved and put into operation. And he endeavored to fill in with surmise the gaps between known events.

After he left the army post, Flint had no doubt learned in Clarksburg of the gold strike to the south and had quickly realized that the strike had been made by the man in whose company he had crossed the desert; the strike he, Flint, would have made had he turned right as he intended to do before the appearance of the hated road runner altered his decision. His mind slightly unhinged by his frightful experience, he had come to hate Tom Ware as the man who had "robbed" him of a fortune. Evidently he had made his way south and had roamed the hills in an endeavor to tap the rich lode from the north. In this he had failed but had hit on the canyon and the cave, which perhaps he explored, and had realized their possibilities. Very likely, sitting by his lonely campfire, muttering in his beard, his single eye glowing like an ember, he worked out the fantastic project to the smallest detail. The plan complete in his mind, he headed for the new town of Coffin and with the embezzled money he carried, opened up his saloon and prospered. But always in his crazed brain seethed his hatred for Tom Ware and determination to get control of the rich property that he felt was rightly his. Shrewd, capable, he knew the importance of building up his influence in the town and country and, being naturally an adroit politician, had succeeded in doing so. He had enlisted the aid of the notorious Graves gang and had suborned, through his love of gambling, the weak Cliff Billings, Tom Ware's mining engineer. Billings' chore being to keep driving the north galleries until the penned up water back of the drift head would be released to flood the mine.

Not without admiration for the capabilities of the mad genius, Slade reviewed his conclusions, which he believed to be in the main correct. He recalled that Robert Flint had first been associated with Edward Duncan at Tucson, Arizona, not far from Tombstone. Perhaps from his familiarity with the watery catastrophe which had doomed the Tombstone silver mines had birthed the germ of the scheme.

What a pity, Slade reflected regretfully, that such a brain should have taken a wrong turn somewhere along the line. And because he chose to ride a crooked trail, Robert Flint or Cole Young, as Slade thought of him, had missed opportunity after opportunity. Had he been honest with his business associate, Edward Duncan, today he would have been a rich man, rich and respected. Had he come forward honestly to congratulate Tom Ware on his good luck, the generous, big-hearted Ware would have handed him a share in the Last Nugget. Indeed, Slade reflected, opportunity knocks not only once at the door of most men's lives but many times. Only all too often not one knock is heeded.

Walt Slade gazed up at the glowing stars whose calm majesty seemed to rebuke the misspent strivings and sordid passions of mankind, and over his soul stole a great peace. Lulled to rest by the clean winds and the silence of the hills, he slept.

CHAPTER 15

Slade awoke at the first primrose streak of dawn. He built up the fire and cooked and ate his breakfast. By the morning light he could see that it was possible to descend to the canyon floor on foot. Leaving Shadow comfortably ensconced in the thicket, he scrambled down to a little strip of beach that flanked the water's edge and approached the cave.

As he expected, it proved to be a limestone formation hollowed out in past ages, probably by the action of water or explosive gases following the path of least resistance. Doubtless it had been driven south through the hill until whatever agent that created it had been balked by the much harder quartz rock which sheathed the limestone cliffs on the south.

The condition of the side walls showed that recently the water level had been considerably higher. Before, of course, a portion of the accumulation in the artificial lake to the north had been drained off into the galleries of the Last Nugget Mine. Now the level would remain static, subject only to fluctuations of the stream that fed the lake and spilled over down the canyon. An ample flow, however, to keep the mine galleries submerged.

Slade penetrated the cave for a short distance, edging along a narrow ledge some three feet above the rushing stream and taking great care not to lose his balance, for a slip would be fatal; no swimmer, however strong, could hope to breast that mill-race of a current which hissed away into the darkness.

Satisfied with what he had learned, he retraced his steps to the open air, climbed the canyon wall and retrieved Shadow. In the blaze of full morning he rode north by east, following the windings of the canyon's lip.

He rode steadily but at a moderate pace, constantly scanning the landscape ahead, for there was no telling what he might encounter. As he drew near the beginning of the lake, he edged away from the canyon rim to where he would be less liable to detection by a chance watcher. Taking advantage of all cover that offered, he proceeded cautiously until he had passed the north mouth of the canyon, into which the stream flowed. He drew rein on the bank of the large creek, almost a river, a couple of hundred yards above where it entered the gorge. Here the stream made an almost right-angle turn, chafing against its rocky shores. And blanketing the turn was a grove of stunted pinons that El Halcon eyed with disfavor; what lay beyond the straggle of trees it was impossible to tell.

Abruptly he sniffed sharply; to his sensitive nostrils had come a faint tang of wood smoke. The Hawk became very much on the alert indeed. Listening and peering, he urged Shadow toward the growth at a slow walk. Suddenly, with bewildering speed, he went sideways out of the saddle; his keen eyes had detected a shadowy drift of movement at the edge of the growth. A bullet yelled past as he struck the ground and the air quivered to the heavy report of a rifle.

Slade hit the ground beside and half behind his horse. Partially concealed by the animal's legs, he lay sprawled and motionless, slitted eyes intent on the clump of trees. Still lying as if he had been knocked from the hull by the slug, he continued to watch the silent growth.

For long moments nothing happened, then he saw a man step cautiously from behind a tree trunk, hesitate an instant, then glide slowly forward, cocked rifle at the ready. He took a dozen slow steps toward the man he thought he had killed. Slade made no move, hoping to take the fellow prisoner and force him to talk. He had no fear, now, of that ready rifle.

The drygulcher continued to advance. He hesitated, came on again, hesitated once more. Then abruptly he seemed to think the motionless body did not look just right. He halted, flinging the rifle to his shoulder.

Slade drew and shot from the hip, again and again and again, the reports blending in a thundering crash.

Blasted by that storm of lead, the man reeled, let his rifle fall and slumped to the ground. Slade leaped erect, smoking gun jutting forward. The drygulcher, game to the last, dragged a gun from its holster, but a slug from Slade's Colt knocked it from his hand. An instant later the Ranger was kneeling beside his writhing form. A single glance at the man's wounds told him death was but a matter of hours, or minutes.

"Anything I can do, fellow?" he asked compassionately.

"Take to cabin — in grove — pull boots off," gasped the stricken man. "Don't want — die — with 'em on!"

He lay back, panting with the effort to speak, blood frothing his lips. Slade picked up his big body as if he were a child and strode into the grove, watchful for possible treachery.

The grove was silent, deserted, and so was

175

the tiny cabin almost hid within the growth. Slade kicked the door open and entered. He laid the drygulcher on a bunk and pulled off his boots. The other gave him a grateful look.

"Told — mother — wouldn't die with — boots on," he mumbled.

"Why'd you try to kill me?" Slade asked gently. "I never did anything to you."

"Orders," croaked the drygulcher. "Orders to shoot anybody what came snoopin' around."

Slade tried a shot in the dark — "Pancho Graves' orders, or Cole Young's? Come clean, fellow, it will make the going easier."

"Young's," gasped the dying man. "He's the big boss; Graves follows his lead. You Tom Ware's man?"

Slade shook his head. The other tried to speak again but sank back, his eyes closing, his breath coming in heavy pants.

Cutting away the man's shirt, Slade bandaged the wounds in his breast. There was very little bleeding, but the Ranger was not fooled by that. Internal hemorrhage was his diagnosis. Doubtful if the poor devil had a chance, but he'd do what he could for him.

He kindled a fire in the rusty stove from a bundle of wood stacked by, noting that some of the kindling was the remains of boxes that had once held dynamite, as the glaring red letters told. He found a bucket and went out for water, whistling Shadow to the cabin and removing his rig. On the bank of the stream he paused, gazing in the last failing light down a narrow, dry gorge past the mouth of which the stream flowed. The floor of the gorge was worn and rutted by swift water, although now it contained none, and littered with smooth boulders and patches of sand. Neither grass nor bush grew among the stones. Dreary, desolate, it stretched westward through the northern flanks of the hills, its smooth walls appearing in the dying light to draw together and join in the distance.

Setting the bucket down on a rock, Slade walked upstream, narrowly examining every inch of the bank. His gray eyes glowed exultantly when finally he returned to the cabin with a filled bucket. He heated water and dressed and rebandaged the drygulcher's wounds, although he knew it was a hopeless task. The man lay white and silent, breathing heavily, his eyes closed. Toward midnight, however, he opened his eyes, saw Slade sitting beside him and smiled faintly.

"You don't hold grudges, do you, feller?" he whispered, his voice little more than a breath of sound. "I'm glad. I'd hate to go out with a man settin' beside me hating me."

Slade leaned closer, and his stern face was suddenly wonderfully gentle, and a little sad.

"Just a question or two, and then I'll let you rest," he said. "When do they blow the dam and return the creek to its original bed?"

The man hesitated, his face clouded with uncertainty. Slade held the famous silver star set on a silver circle before the dying man's eyes.

The drygulcher stared with his almost fixed eyes, tried to raise his body.

"A Ranger!" he gasped at last. "Feller, are you a *Ranger?*"

"Yes," El Halcon told him gently. "With Captain McNelty's company. I ride the straight trail, and I'm giving you a last chance to ride it with me."

The glazing eyes brightened. "I'll ride, Ranger," the outlaw whispered. "They'll blow the dam right after they break through into the mine with the tunnel at Coffin. I'm to get word when to light the fuse."

"And when the water is drained from the mine and the artificial lake up here emptied, the flow will stop?" Slade prompted.

"That's — right."

The heaving chest fell in, the tired eyes

closed. But they opened again for an instant, and the ghost of a smile flickered across their surface. "Trail's end, Ranger — crooked trail — with a *straight ending!*"

Walt Slade bowed his black head and his lips moved silently. In a tree outside the cabin some night bird sounded a liquid note, and again, and yet again, like to the measured throb of a "passing" bell.

Slade raised his eyes to the dark square of the window, beyond which, high in the blue-black velvet of the sky, a great star glowed and trembled.

"Once upon a time a thief who repented on a Cross was promised Paradise," he said aloud. "Wouldn't be surprised if there's enough 'last minute' mercy left for still another."

CHAPTER 16

There were tools in the cabin and with pick and shovel Slade dug a grave and buried the dead man, wrapped in a blanket from one of the bunks, in the first light of morning. He did not mound the grave but smoothed it over and carefully replaced the sod he had cut out. When he finished there was no trace of the fellow's last resting place which he marked for his own identification by the position of certain trees relative to the grave.

After finishing the task he walked up the stream to where a rude but efficient dam had been constructed to divert the creek from its original bed down the narrow gorge into the broader canyon. The ingenuity with which the dam had been placed so as to provide a spillway into the canyon, the floor of which was at a somewhat greater elevation than that of the gorge, attested to Cole Young's engineering ingenuity. And attested even greater, Slade thought, to his persuasive genius in being able to get such a bunch as the Graves gang to do such a chore of hard work.

After an extensive search, Slade discovered the dynamite charges that would blow out the dam and send the creek back to its former course. They were capped and fused with waterproofed fuses and all ready for firing. For some time he stood lost in study, then he got the rig on Shadow, mounted him and set out for the lower end of the lake.

The dam which had been set in the narrow neck of the canyon to assist in compounding the waters of the lake had been a simpler matter but had also entailed plenty of hard work. It, of course, had been blown when the water backed up in the great cave and broken into the Last Nugget mine. Slade shook his head in admiration of Cole Young's meticulous attention to detail. Quite likely the water imprisoned in the cave would have been sufficient to flood the mine, but Young had taken no chances and had also constructed the reservoir which was the lake to give an additional head if needed.

Lounging in the saddle, Slade rolled a cigarette and pondered the situation. He had ready to hand all that was necessary to enable Tom Ware to recover the valuable mining property that had been filched from him by fraud; that angle was properly taken care of. But his duty as a Ranger was not so simple. For he still had no case against Cole Young or Pancho Graves. The lips of the outlaw who told him that Young and Graves engineered the scheme were sealed by death. Young could disavow any connection with the affair and it was highly probable that a good lawyer would win an acquittal for him if Slade tried to prefer charges.

And Walt Slade was grimly determined that Cole Young should not go free. He was a potential murderer, no less. Only Slade's foresight in suggesting that a drill be driven three feet ahead of the drift head as a safety precaution had saved a dozen men from death by drowning. Cole Young, a competent engineer, must have known what would be the probable results when the water suddenly broke through into the mine; only a miracle could have saved the men working the drift head. They would have been drowned like rats in a flushed drain.

So Slade's chore wasn't finished yet, not by a jugful! He still had to entrap Young and his vicious allies. Sitting his tall black horse, the Ranger who had been called the most fearless and capable of all that illustrious corps of fearless and capable men thought it out and evolved a plan he believed would work. With an easier mind he set out for Coffin, leading the dead outlaw's horse, saddled and bridled, which he had discovered under a leanto back of the cabin. Later he would remove the rig, hide it and turn the animal loose to fend for itself, which it could do without suffering until somebody picked it up.

Slade knew perfectly well that the plan involved great personal danger to himself. One slip would mean failure and, very likely, an end to his interest in mundane affairs. Pancho Graves was vicious as a Gila monster, Blaine Gulden a cold killer, and Cole Young even more to be reckoned with because he had more brains.

But such were the hazards of his occupation and he dismissed them with a shrug, just as he dismissed the treacherous attempt on his life at the site of Robert Flint's old camp. His real concern was for the success or failure of the plan destined to bring law breakers to justice. That was paramount where a Ranger was concerned. Cole Young and his associates had flouted their country's laws and must be punished and, one way or another, taken care of so that they could no longer do so.

Upon arriving at Coffin, Slade immediately hunted up Tom Ware and laid the facts before him. Ware listened in angry amazement.

"I've a notion to go over to that blasted saloon and shoot Cole Young," he declared wrathfully. But Slade vetoed the suggestion.

"Would very likely just get you killed and do little good," he explained. "Also, it would allow the rest of the bunch to escape. We still have nothing against them that would stand up in court. Taking the law in your own hands is always bad business and would be particularly so in this instance. We've got to move carefully and shrewdly. Young has brains and any little slip will arouse his suspicions and enable him to slide from under. I think I've figured a way to trap him and the others. But I repeat, we've got to move carefully and consider all the angles. Unfortunately, I can't be in two or three places at once so I'll have to have help. I gather Town Marshal Jim Lowe is an honest man and capable. As Town Marshal he has no official authority outside of Coffin, but I'll deputize him and that will give him all he needs. We'll need four or five more good men who can shoot."

"No worry about that," said Ware. "I'll take care of it."

"That'll be fine," said Slade. "We'll have to wait until Young breaks through into the mine and the water begins to flow through his tunnel. I hope it'll be soon, against the possibility of somebody visiting that cabin in the grove."

"Should happen any day now," said Ware. "Water's coming through the rock."

"That's good," Slade nodded. "When the water breaks through, Young will send a messenger to the man supposed to be in on guard at the dam with word to blow the dam and send the creek back into its original channel. The water in the mine will drain off and part of that impounded in the artificial lake. Most of the lake, however, will flow back into the creek for the floor of the canyon is of slightly higher elevation than that of the gorge which is the creek's natural channel. We've got to intercept that messenger so he won't get back to Young with word that something is wrong."

"I'd like that chore," grunted Ware, "for I suppose you'll want Young for your own meat."

"In a way, yes," Slade smiled. "Or at least I think I'd better give him my personal attention. I've had some experience with his sort and I imagine I'm better equipped than most to handle that chore."

"That I don't doubt," conceded Ware. "But how about the messenger?"

"I think it would be a good notion for you and another husky or two to hole up in that cabin and grab him when he shows," Slade decided. "Try and get him alive if possible; tie him up and guard him. We may need somebody to do a little talking before this affair is finished."

"I can understand that," grunted Ware. "Don't worry, I'll take care of the sidewinder. And now I suppose the only thing we can do for the present is sit tight and wait for Young to break through into the mine. I'll get in touch with the boys and Marshal Lowe and have them at my place tonight — you know where it is, over on

Prescott Street. I suppose you'll be there?"

"Yes," Slade replied. "I'll deputize everybody. And I want them to meet there the night of the day the water comes through. Suppose it won't attract any attention?"

"Not a bit," declared Ware. "The boys have been dropping over all the time since the trouble started, to discuss ways and means of combating it. Nobody will think anything of them being there at any time."

"That's fine," said Slade. "Now let's drop around to Manuel's place for something to eat; I've been living on short rations for the past couple of days."

Slade was pleased to see that the old *cantina* owner treated Tom Ware with the same deference he had accorded him in his more prosperous days, and he was of the opinion that Manuel wouldn't lose anything by so doing once Ware was on his feet again, which would be soon.

In the canyon where Cole Young was driving his tunnel was great activity and an air of expectancy. Water was coming into the tunnel faster than the day before. Young himself was superintending the work and proving to anybody conversant with such matters what a skilled engineer he was. The engineers from the other mines, who spent all their spare time in the canyon, regarded him with puzzled astonishment.

"That one-eyed hellion knows his business," was the general agreement. "Wonder where the devil he learned it? I'd give something pretty to know where he came from and why he went into the saloon business, with his knowledge and ability."

"Well, boys, I'd say that question isn't so hard to answer," a grizzled old-timer observed dryly. "We have considerable knowledge and ability also, in our particular line, but we're still working for wages while Young is a highly prosperous and influential citizen and, if he *should* happen to be right in what he's doing, not that I'm admitting for a moment that he is, he stands to cash in mighty big winnings on his gamble. And if he loses, I guess he can afford to lose what it would take one of us a couple of years to earn. Does that answer your question, McLoughlin?"

"Guess it does," the other engineer grinned. "Sort of looks like Young was smart to get into the saloon business."

The following morning, Slade rode to the canyon. He studied the tunneling operations a few minutes and then returned to town.

"Not today," he told Tom Ware.

"How can you be so sure?" Ware asked.

"Because Cole Young knows his business," Slade replied. "He hasn't moved his excavating machinery out of the tunnel; he knows there'll be no break-through today or he would have made preparations for setting his final blasts."

"Wonder where the devil that horned toad got the notion to do what he's doing," Ware remarked.

"Very likely he got his inspiration from what happened to the Tombstone mines," Slade explained. "According to what Edward Duncan said, Young, or Robert Flint, as he was known then, was at Tucson, a comparative short distance from Tombstone, when the Tombstone mines were flooded. He must have been thoroughly conversant with what happened and while exploring the hills to the north, the incident recurred to him and he saw a way for a 'repetition' of what happened at Tombstone. At least that's my guess."

"I've a notion you're right," Ware admitted.

The next day was a repetition of the one preceding it and Walt Slade began to grow acutely nervous. There was always the chance of one of Pancho Graves' men riding up to the cabin by the lake, to relieve the watchman there or for some other purpose.

Should one do so and find the watchman missing, suspicion would very probably be aroused and Slade's carefully worked out plan be badly scrambled.

"But there's nothing we can do but wait," he told the gathering at Tom Ware's house that night. "We're all set to go, but we can't make a move till the water starts to flow from the mine."

"This blasted waiting is the worst part of the business," Tom Ware growled as he paced the floor with jerky steps. "I want action!"

"You'll very likely get it, till it runs out of your ears," Slade chuckled. "Just tighten your cinches and take it easy."

"I don't believe you've got a nerve in your body," the mine owner snorted. "You don't seem to pay any more mind to what's ahead of us than if it was a trip to the general store."

"General stores can be dangerous," Slade replied cheerfully. "Folks have been known to get poisoned from what they bought there."

Ware snorted again and resumed his pacing.

One more nerve tightening day followed, and then things began to move. The next morning Young was clearing his machinery from the tunnel. The word that the final blasts were set to go got around quickly, and very soon the majority of Coffin's inhabitants were clustered on the higher ground near the canyon walls. Slade noted that Pancho Graves and Blaine Gulden were with Young in a group near the tunnel mouth. Sheriff John Blount bustled about importantly.

The tunnel mouth itself was deserted and yawned black and silent save for the gurgling of water in the drainage ditches. Back in its dark depths, powder men were busy setting the charges for the blasts that would bring down the last barrier to the water in the drowned Last Nugget mine.

Tom Ware was not among those present in the canyon, and only Walt Slade knew that at the moment Ware and two companions were speeding north up the west fork of the draw.

Suddenly men came darting from the tunnel mouth. The crowd shouted, then abruptly was very still.

Deep in the bowels of the earth sounded a muffled boom, another and another; there was an instant of tingling suspense. Then the air vibrated to a pulsing murmur that swiftly rose to a sullen roar. Out of the tunnel thundered a torrent of inky water. It filled the tunnel from the floor to roof, gushing and frothing as from the nozzle of a giant hose pipe. Into the channel prepared for it stormed the flood, rolling swiftly down the canyon to lose itself in the desert sands.

The crowd whooped and cheered. Cole Young's single eye gleamed with malicious triumph.

Hour after hour the water poured forth with unabated violence. Cole Young continued to smile.

"But it'll keep coming," declared the engineers of the other mines. "That water is under terrific pressure, and water's still flowing from the mine tunnel up in the draw. The in-take is greater than the outflow; you can't even drain the upper workings, for the gallery you tapped can't accommodate the flow."

"Wait and see," replied Young. "She'll run all day today and all tonight and part of tomorrow, but by the middle of the afternoon tomorrow there'll be nothing but a trickle the pumps can take care of."

The engineers looked at one another. The skill with which Cole Young had outlined and directed the tunneling convinced them that he was an experienced and competent engineer; as such he should know better. He was talking arrant nonsense. If merely a reservoir of accumulated water back in the rock had been tapped, the flow would already be lessening, but it wasn't. The flood still thundered from the tunnel and showed no indications of abating.

Yes, Young was talking nonsense, but his smug complacency rendered them a bit uneasy. What card *did* the shrewd devil have up his sleeve?

All that day and all night the water roared from the tunnel, and all the next morning. But as the afternoon wore on, to Young's incredulous amazement, it continued to roar. The mine engineers chortled with triumph but didn't get a chance to twit Young over his blunder. Young was not in the canyon.

Chapter 17

There was hurried and stormy consultation in the back room of Cole Young's Square Deal saloon. Pancho Graves and Blaine Gulden were there with their hard-faced men. And Sheriff Jim Blount, nervously pacing the floor, his mouth twitching.

"Chances are there was just a little slip-up that means nothing," Pancho Graves observed reassuringly. "Holmes up at the cabin may have been out hunting or something and wasn't there when Harvey showed up with the word to blow the dam. Or maybe Harvey met with an accident of some sort that delayed him; such things happen in the hills."

"Maybe," whined Sheriff Blount, "but I'm worried. Ever since that infernal El Halcon showed up here there's been trouble. That hellion gives me the creeps. When he looked at me that day in the saloon I felt he was looking right through me rather than at me. His eyes made me feel all crawled-up inside. I remember coming around a turn in a trail once, a mighty narrow trail with a cliff on one side and a drop into a canyon on the other, and there was a mountain lion coming around in the other direction. He looked me plumb in the face, and when El Halcon looked at me the day I met him here in the saloon, the first thing I thought of was that lion, and I got just the same kind of a crawl inside. If he's onto us, we ain't safe."

"I still think the best thing would have been for me to pick a row with him and have a showdown," said Blaine Gulden.

"You'd have just got yourself killed and accomplished nothing," replied Pancho Graves. "You're good, but not good enough to pull with El Halcon. Oh, I know you're itching to try conclusions with him, and

I hope you get the chance — with things rigged to give you something like an even break. You wouldn't have a show otherwise."

Cole Young who had been brooding at the end of the table spoke for the first time.

"All this palaver is getting us exactly nowhere," he said. "Something went wrong, although I can't imagine what; we've got to learn just what did or didn't happen and why. Graves, an hour after dark, you and your men head for that cabin. Blount, you go with them. You'd better slip out of town first and wait for them above where the draw forks. You don't want to be seen riding with them. And be careful, Graves, and don't barge into something; keep your eyes open."

"You figure El Halcon might be holed up in that cabin?" Graves asked.

"Could be," Young conceded, "but I've a notion you fellows can handle him."

"You're darn right," Blaine Gulden growled.

"You're staying here with me, Gulden," Young said, "in case there's something at this end of the line that needs looking after. Now take it easy and don't get jumpy. We're not going to be outsmarted by one brush-popping outlaw no matter how good he is.

194

What the devil are you smirking about, Gulden?"

"I was just thinking," Gulden chuckled, "what a joke it would be if when the Last Nugget miners broke through the drift head in the mine, they really did tap a big underground river like they did over at Tombstone. Yes, the joke would be on us for fair, and on El Halcon, too, if he figures to horn in and cut himself a share."

"You're crazy as popcorn on a red hot stove!" scoffed Young. "I explored all the cracks and crevices in those limestone cliffs that butt up against the quartz formations on the north. They're dry as a bone and have been for ages. I know my business, Gulden."

"Hope so," said Gulden. "If you don't — well, I hope you do."

An hour after dark, Pancho Graves and his men did ride north. At the forks of the draw, nervous Sheriff Blount joined them. They didn't know it, but far ahead rode Town Marshal Jim Lowe and six grim old former plainsmen who could dot a lizard's eye with a sixgun at ten paces.

Back in the Square Deal rear room, Blaine Gulden turned to Young. "Cole, just why did you send Graves and the boys on ahead like you did, and keep me back?"

"Well," Young replied dryly, "if something *is* wrong up there, let them run into it. We'll mosey along later and be in a position to get the upper hand no matter what happens to Graves and his bunch. Doesn't that make sense to you?"

"Yes, I guess it does," Gulden said slowly. "You're not worried much about Graves and the boys, are you?"

"Not a bit," Young replied. "Graves is stupid and so are the rest of them. They've just about served their turn and what happens to them from now on doesn't concern me."

"And there would be fewer to divide with, eh?" Gulden said softly. "Cole, that *does* make sense."

Pancho Graves and his men rode steadily at a good pace until they neared the grove in which the cabin sat; then they reduced their speed and crept along with the greatest caution, halting in the shadow of a thicket when they sighted the clump of pinons.

The trees stood black and motionless in the brilliant moonlight and the only sound to be heard was that of the rushing waters of the creek worrying against its stony banks. No gleam of light showed between the trunks.

For long minutes the little group of outlaws sat their horses, peering and listening. Then they moved forward once more until they reached the outer straggle of trees between which grew thick underbrush. Here Graves again called a halt.

"Somehow I don't like the looks of things," he whispered to his companions. "Things are too blasted dark and quiet. If Holmes and Harvey are there, it seems they'd have a light burning. We're not taking chances we don't have to. If something is off-color in that shack we'll find out before we go barging up to it."

He beckoned a lithe, swarthy man, a "breed" of almost, but not quite, pure Yaqui blood.

"Felipe," he told him, "you're about as good a tracker as there is in Texas and you know how to see without being seen. Slide along through the trees and give things a once-over. If everything doesn't look right, slip back and let us know and we'll try and figure what to do."

The breed dismounted and a moment later melted silently into the deeper darkness beneath the trees. He advanced in utter silence, pausing from time to time to peer and listen. It took him many minutes to reach a point where he could get a view of the dark cabin. A tiny rustling beside him caused him to stiffen, hand streaking to his gun.

But before he could draw it, a pistol barrel crunched against his skull and he slumped to the ground with a choking gasp and lay motionless.

Marshal Jim Lowe stepped from behind the tree trunk beside which Felipe had paused, holstering his Colt, the barrel of which was bloodied. From the shelter of other trunks and clumps of brush appeared alert, hard-eyed men, including Tom Ware, with ready rifles in their hands.

"He's knocked out, but tie him and shove a gag in his mouth," whispered the marshal. "Okay? Come along, then, and no noise. Slade had it right when he said the bunch would halt beyond the trees and send somebody on foot to look things over. Easy, now, no noise, and let me do the talking, if there's any talking to do."

The posse crept forward noiselessly. Behind a final fringe of undergrowth they dropped to hands and knees and wormed ahead like so many purposeful snakes.

At the edge of the grove, Pancho Graves and his men lounged comfortably in their saddles, waiting the return of Felipe; Pancho himself was rolling a cigarette. A strangled squawk from fat Sheriff Blount jerked his head up. Paper and tobacco fluffed into the air as Graves made a desperate grab for his gun. He never got it.

Marshal Lowe's Colt cracked and Graves howled a bitter oath and wrung his bloody fingers. Still cursing, he slowly raised his hands shoulder high. His smugglers, pasty under their tan, already had their hands up, cowed by the unswerving rifle barrels and the grim faces behind them. Fat John Blount wailed like a lost soul with the pip.

"That's right," said the marshal, "and don't try anything. The next one will be dead center. Unfork with your hands up."

The outlaws obeyed, Graves still mouthing and muttering, Blount quavering unintelligibly.

"Get their hardware, boys," ordered the marshal, "then herd 'em along to the cabin. Say! we're short one! Gulden isn't here. Where is he, Graves? Talk, or I'll pistol whip you within an inch of your ornery life!"

"He's back in town, he didn't come along," Graves mouthed sullenly.

"With Young?"

"That's right."

Marshal Lowe fingered his gun, a worried expression on his face.

"I'm bothered about Slade," he said to Tom Ware. "Gulden is dangerous, the worst of the lot. Slade said he'd be here later, but what if he slipped up somehow?"

"I don't think you need worry about Slade slipping up on anything," Ware replied dryly. "He said for us to wait for him in the cabin and we'll do just that. A couple of you bring along the horses, boys. All right, you horned toads, march!"

Two hours after Pancho Graves and his smugglers headed north, Cole Young and Blaine Gulden slipped out the back door of the Square Deal saloon, secured their horses and left Coffin by way of little used streets. They turned into the west fork of the draw and also rode north.

And behind them drifted a shadow, trailing them as only El Halcon could trail a quarry.

Young and Gulden rode at an easy but steady pace. Slade, now familiar with the route, kept well in the rear, sighting the pair only when they topped a rise or when he himself reached the crest of a ridge and saw them riding below in the brilliant moonlight. But as they drew near the grove, he closed the distance as much as possible.

Slade wondered if Marshal Lowe and his

posse had been successful with Pancho Graves and his smugglers. Lowe was an experienced peace officer, but Graves was a smooth article and would take advantage of any slip the marshal might make. And Slade knew well that if there had been a slip, he, Slade would not be likely to learn the details in this world. He'd very probably find himself surrounded when he followed Young and Gulden to the edge of the grove. And he was more than a little puzzled over why Young and Graves' chief lieutenant hadn't ridden north with the others. The business had a queer look. But just the same he closed the distance more and more.

He saw Young and Gulden pull up before they reached the trees, dismount and circle the grove toward the bank of the stream slightly above it, where the dynamite charges designed to blow out the dam were set. He in turn unforked and, taking advantage of every scrap of cover, closed in on the unsuspecting pair.

Where the stream bank sloped toward the desolate, boulder-strewn gorge that wound away into the west, Young and Gulden halted, staring at the rushing water.

"It hasn't been touched," muttered Gulden. "The charges are still in place. Cole, this is almighty funny."

"No, it's almighty serious," hissed Cole Young. "Blaine, it's a trap! Fork your bronc and ride!"

The two whirled toward their horses, then recoiled. Between them and the animals stood Walt Slade, thumbs hooked over his double cartridge belts, the star of the Rangers gleaming on his broad breast. His voice rolled forth, "In the name of the State of Texas! I arrest for fraud, robbery and attempted murder, Blaine Gulden and — *Robert Flint!*"

With a strangled gasp, Cole Young fell back at the words. Gulden stood for an instant like a bronze statue. Then his supple hands flashed down.

He was fast, very fast, but Slade drew and shot him before his guns cleared leather. With the guns in his shaking hands, vainly trying to steady his tortured muscles, he went down, his chest smashed and splintered by the Ranger's bullets. Cole Young, who had been Robert Flint, embezzler and thief, managed to fire once, wildly, before Slade's bullet laced through his heart.

Holstering his smoking Colts, Slade walked to the fallen men. Young was dead, but Blaine Gulden, his dark face still saturninely handsome, managed the glimmer of a smile.

"Graves was right — I wasn't — good enough!" he whispered as his eyes closed.

Down in the grove, the cabin door banged open. Shouts sounded, drawing swiftly nearer. Slade made sure he recognized Tom Ware's stentorian bellow before he made his presence known.

"Okay," he called. "Everything's under control. Come ahead."

A moment later the posse hove into view, Tom Ware in the lead.

"Are you all right, son?" he called anxiously.

"Fine as frog hair," Slade replied.

The posse grouped around the two bodies, chattering excitedly. Ware stopped to peer into Cole Young's dead face.

"Looks like we made a clean sweep," he chortled. "We got the rest of the sidewinders corraled in the cabin. Got the drop on them and they came along like lambs."

Slade ran his eyes over those present. "Say!" he exclaimed. "Didn't anybody stay behind to keep a watch on the prisoners?"

"Oh, they're safe enough," Ware replied. "We hogtied 'em."

"But they may not stay hogtied," Slade said. "Come on, let's get back down there in a hurry."

CHAPTER 18

Felipe, the wily little breed, wasn't hit as hard as Marshal Lowe thought. The blow which split his scalp had been a glancing one and Felipe, in fact, was only stunned and had gotten his senses back by the time the possemen finished tieing and gagging him. But with *Indio* cunning, he feigned unconsciousness and began working industriously with supple wrists and almost prehensile fingers to free himself of his bonds. By the time he was carried into the cabin and deposited on the floor in a corner he had the knots so loosened that he would be able to quickly wriggle loose. He lay biding his time and awaiting an opportunity.

When the posse pounded out of the cabin and raced in the direction of the shooting upstream, Felipe jerked his hands free. The possemen had relieved him of his gun but overlooked the knife hung by a thong down the back of his neck. Felipe whipped the knife from its sheath and began slashing the cords that bound his companions.

Freed, the outlaws dived for their hardware, which had been stacked on a table. Fully armed, they made a rush for their horses which, still saddled and bridled, were tethered outside the cabin. They had loosed the animals and were starting to mount when the returning posse burst from the trees. Instantly the little clearing in which the cabin stood fairly exploded with a bellow of gunfire.

Back and forth through the wan moonlight spurted the orange flashes. A posseman pitched forward on his face, another doubled up with a choking grunt. Still a third yelled shrilly as a bullet smashed his shoulder.

Walt Slade, blood streaming down his face from a nicked scalp, was shooting with both hands. He fired point-blank at an outlaw who had lined sights with Tom Ware, saw the man writhe and fall. A slug grazed his temple and hurled him sideways with the shock, red flashes spinning before his eyes. He steadied himself and downed the man who fired it. He tried desperately for a shot at Pancho Graves who kept dodging behind the others.

One by one the outlaws went down, fighting furiously to the last. All but one, who managed to mount his frantic horse and send the animal speeding toward the trees; it was Pancho Graves.

Slade lined sights with the fleeing smuggler chief but when he pulled trigger, the hammer clicked on an empty shell. Graves vanished into the brush. Slade ran forward, stuffing fresh cartridges into the cylinders of his empty guns and whistling a clear loud note.

There was a crashing in the brush and a moment later Shadow hove into view, snorting and blowing. Slade holstered his guns and swung into the saddle, but when he cleared the grove and sighted Graves, the outlaw was a good half mile ahead.

But there was only one way that Graves could go and the brilliant moonlight made the scene almost as bright as day. Slade settled himself in the saddle and gave Shadow his head.

He soon realized, however, that the tall black had his work cut out for him. Graves' big dun was a splendid animal, almost, though not quite, as fast as Shadow. But Slade was confident he didn't have Shadow's staying powers and that it was only a matter of time. That is, if he could overtake the outlaw before he reached the tangle of benches and gullies farther down the draw. Once in that misty maze, Graves might easily lose his pursuer.

On sped the dun horse, now lost in the shadow, now seen again where the moonshine poured down in a silver flood. Slade estimated the distance and loosened his

Winchester in the saddle boot. Before long, if Shadow kept gaining, he could risk a shot. Not too soon, however, for if he was to hope for the bullet to reach its mark, Shadow would have to level off in his smooth running walk, which meant the sacrifice of some of his speed and as it was, he was traveling only slightly faster than the dun.

Mile after mile streamed past under the flying hoofs, and minute by minute Shadow closed the distance. Graves glanced back, his face a gray blur in the moonlight. He settled himself more firmly in the saddle and bent low over his mount's neck, affording a very dubious target in the deceptive light.

And ahead, not more than a mile distant, began the series of benches and the brush choked gulleys into which they led. Slade urged Shadow to greater speed.

The dun flashed onto one of the benches, the very one, in fact, on which Robert Flint fought his battle with the Apaches. Slade drew the Winchester and clamped the butt against his shoulder.

"Steady!" he told Shadow. The black horse leveled off; Slade squeezed the trigger.

He saw Graves duck and knew the bullet must have come close. He steadied the rifle for another shot.

Graves glanced back; whirled his mount and sent it charging for the lip of the bench; he was going to risk a jump to the second bench some twenty feet below. Slade's finger tightened on the trigger, but before he could fire, the dun took the jump, soaring through space like a bird. But when he hit the ground below, he stumbled and went end over end like a plugged rabbit. Graves was thrown high into the air. He struck the rocky surface of the bench with an awesome thud, twitched a moment and lay still. Slade pulled his foaming horse to a halt and gazed at the two bodies lying stark and motionless in the moonlight. Little doubt but that the terrific fall had broken both necks.

But Slade had to make sure. He sent Shadow along the bench until he found a spot where it was possible to descend without suffering a similar fate. A few minutes later he paused beside the bodies.

Graves was dead, his head twisted around at a horrible angle, until he appeared to be looking straight back over his shoulder. The horse had also died instantly.

Slade gazed at the silent forms for a moment, then turned and headed back for the cabin in the grove. Before he had covered half the distance he met Tom Ware riding at top speed.

"Was afraid you might have trouble with the hellion and figured I'd better come see," he said as he pulled up alongside Slade. "What happened?"

Slade told him. Ware nodded his head with satisfaction.

"Looks like we finally did just about make a clean sweep," he said. "All but fat John Blount. He was lying on the ground playing possum; didn't have a scratch. Been gabbin' his head off ever since. You were right in every detail."

"How about our boys?" Slade asked.

"We lost two men," Ware returned sadly. "A couple more got punctured, but we patched them up and they can ride. Now what's next in line?"

"Next we'll blow that dam and return the creek to its natural channel," Slade said. "The lake will quickly empty, its bed being slightly higher than the floor of the gorge through which the creek formerly ran. By the time we get back to town the mine should have drained and you can take over the property filched from you by fraud and start production again."

Full daylight had broken when they reached the cabin in the grove. The wounded men had been made as comfortable as conditions permitted and the bodies laid out. Fat John Blount was still talking and nobody was paying him any mind. Slade, however, paused to ask him a few questions, which the frightened sheriff answered volubly and in detail.

The Ranger was chuckling when he rejoined Tom Ware. "It would appear that, inadvertently, as it were, I succeeded in clearing up that which brought me to this section in the first place," he explained his amusement. "Pancho Graves was smuggling arms and ammunition across the Rio Grande to troublemakers in Mexico, and Cole Young was procuring them for him. Well, they won't smuggle any more!"

Without delay, Slade proceeded to light the charges set to blow the dam. Following the boom of the dynamite was the roar of the artificial lake pouring into the gorge to swell the creek almost to the crest of its high banks.

Slade watched the rushing water for a while then repaired to the cabin, where he procured a pick and shovel. He located the spot where the drygulcher who at the last moment turned to the straight trail slept peacefully in his lonely grave. Removing the sod with which he had hidden the outlaw's last resting place, he mounded the grave and set a simple headboard in place, on which he carved with his knife, *Went Out Like a Man.*

The bodies of the outlaws and the slain possemen were strapped to the backs of horses and the grim cavalcade set out for town, pausing to pick up that of Pancho Graves' and take it along with the others, arriving at Coffin in the late evening.

Great was the excitement when the story got around. Slade was showered with congratulations.

"When the water stopped running out of that tunnel we were plumb flabbergasted," one of the mine engineers told him. "Looked like Cole Young was right with all the odds against him. Sort of a relief to have what we said would happen backed up, as it were. We were beginning to wonder if we hadn't better go back to school and learn the business all over."

That night the sirens of every mine and mill were tied down for a full half hour. Pistols cracked, charges of dynamite set off up the gulch boomed, and every man who had any respect for himself got drunk!

That is with a few exceptions. Walt Slade and the exhausted possemen didn't get drunk. They went to bed early and slept the sleep of the just.

The following morning Slade had breakfast with Tom Ware at old Manuel's restaurant. The ancient Mexican was heartbroken at the thought of Slade leaving and said so with tears in his eyes.

"And I sure wish you'd stay and help me get things going again," said Tom Ware. "I'll give you charge of the mine — I'm short an engineer, you know. Cliff Billings hightailed for parts unknown. Good riddance! He was mixed up in it, all right. Understand he was heavily in debt to Young for gambling losses."

"That's how Young got him under his thumb and made him go along with the scheme," Slade replied. "Billings kept the work of driving the galleries north going ahead in the face of complaints by the stamp-mill manager, although he knew well, of course, that the rock brought down there was practically worthless and would continue to be so."

"The rapscallion had me fooled, all right," said Ware. "I trusted him and figured he knew his business."

"Oh, he knew his business, all right," Slade smiled. "Which was to pull the wool over your eyes and lay the ground work for Young's crooked manipulations. But don't let that bother you. You're not an engineer and Billings was smart enough to be able to keep the engineers of the other mines from becoming suspicious."

"Reckon that's so," Ware admitted. "And you're sure you won't stay? You've earned a slice in the property, and you'll get it."

Walt Slade smilingly shook his head. "I'm a Ranger and expect to continue being one for a while yet," he declined. "And the kind of a town you'll be running from now on won't need any Rangers."

"*Thanks* to the Rangers," interpolated Tom Ware.

"So I'll be riding," Slade continued. "I want to get word of what happened to Captain Jim, pronto, so he can notify Edward Duncan of Bob Flint's death and get that ten thousand dollar fund for the needy dependents of dead Rangers set up and operating. And he'll have another little chore ready for me, the chances are, by the time I get back to the post."

Tom Ware and old Manuel watched him ride away, tall and graceful atop his great black horse, to where duty called and danger and new adventure waited.

And back around a bend in the trail came his glorious golden voice in a hauntingly beautiful song of the range.

We hope you have enjoyed this Large Print book. Other Thorndike, Wheeler, Kennebec, and Chivers Press Large Print books are available at your library or directly from the publishers.

For information about current and upcoming titles, please call or write, without obligation, to:

Publisher
Thorndike Press
295 Kennedy Memorial Drive
Waterville, ME 04901
Tel. (800) 223-1244

or visit our Web site at:

http://gale.cengage.com/thorndike

OR

Chivers Large Print
published by BBC Audiobooks Ltd
St James House, The Square
Lower Bristol Road
Bath BA2 3SB
England
Tel. +44(0) 800 136919
email: bbcaudiobooks@bbc.co.uk
www.bbcaudiobooks.co.uk

All our Large Print titles are designed for easy reading, and all our books are made to last.